Nighthawk Alley

NIGHTHAWK ALLEY

Anthony Glavin

NEW ISLAND BOOKS

Dublin

Nighthawk Alley
is first published in 1997
in Ireland by
New Island Books,
2 Brookside,
Dundrum Road,
Dublin 14,
Ireland.

ISBN 1 874597 68 5

New Island Books receives financial assistance from
The Arts Council (An Chomhairle Ealaíon),
Dublin, Ireland.

Cover design by Jon Berkeley
Typeset by Yellowstone
Printed in Ireland by Colour Books, Ltd.

For Adrienne

SPRING

I KNEW Fintan was a piece of work the day I hired him. "There's no bowling team here?" he jokes, as I toss him a pair of coveralls off a nail in the garage. Maybe it was a case of one spider knows another — both of us Irish? Only I'm a garden variety model, while Fintan's more a brightly coloured tropical job, like on Maggie's nature programmes. He isn't that exotic to look at, mind you. Apart from a silver earring which gives me a moment's pause. Slight, medium-height, sandy-haired, around thirty. Nothing that pass-remarkable, though you'd notice the lively green eyes. And the purple Doc Martens maybe. "No bowling team unless you start one," I tell him. "Meantime you start at seven tomorrow."

He shows up at seven too, which itself is unusual for Irish. Not that anybody, Italian or Puerto Rican, is much better these days. Not that I've ever taken on a PR, mind you. The Greek kid I have helping out is often late. But Evangelis is probably on Chinese time, anyways, crazy about karate.

Anyhow, it's slow that first morning, even at the pumps, and by noon I lose sight of Fintan. Just when I have him figured for a half-day wonder, I spy him in a corner of our lot beside the alley that runs between us and the three-storey tenement next door, picking up trash from the overgrown grass. Now while I garden at home myself, I don't even bother to police that patch of weeds and dog shit. Sometimes a bum pushing a supermarket cart with a bit of copper piping for the scrap-yard pokes through the rotting leaves. Looking for beer bottles or soda cans worth a nickel deposit each. But I only use that lot to park the garage loaner, and the odd used car I'm trying to shift.

"Any money is mine," I say when Fintan comes back into the tiny office, which doubles as a waiting room.

"Have you a grass hook?" he asks.

"Jaysus, you'll want a lawn mower next!"

"A scythe," he replies, reminding me he's a culchie at heart. From the arse end of Donegal, he'd told me the day before, when he inquired about a start.

"Ballantine, Canadian Club, Southern Comfort," he reels off. "Four Feathers, and Old Thompson," tipping the empty bottles he collected into the bin.

"This Paddy is langers," I tell him. "Sitting outside the parochial house, when the priest comes out. 'What's that you have in the paper bag, Paddy?'

"'Oh, just a bottle of Four Fathers, Feather!'"

In reply Fintan tells me one about a young widow at confession.

"What's Old Thompson?" he later asks.

"Northern Comfort," I tell him. Explaining it's a favourite Boston whiskey. "Cheap at half the price."

I ask a few questions about Donegal, which he left nearly ten years back. It seems he worked in London, then Germany, before coming to the States around five years ago. Mostly he's been knocking about all over, Florida, California and Arizona, places I know only from television. Donegal I don't know either, but then he doesn't know Dublin. Not that I do anymore, as I've been nearly thirty years here, and it's ten years since I last went back for a visit.

Fintan says he first learned about cars by stripping and reassembling his uncle's Morris Minor, like an Army rifle, in the thatched shed behind the uncle's cottage. "He'd an old Ford tractor too, which I got to drive when my father needed to bring turf down off the hill. My uncle wouldn't let my father near it, after he turned it over once, coming down the Green Bank." I always notice that about culchies — the way they talk about the "Green Bank" or the "wee strand", like they're pubs or post offices or proper banks. Landmarks, like.

Fintan is the same way about the rest room as the grass lot, I discover a few days later. "What are you using on the toilet bowl?" I inquire, barely recognizing it.

"Coca-Cola," he tells me.

"I'll buy some Ajax," I say. "So you won't be out of pocket."

"Not to worry, Mickey," he says. "I was buying the Cokes out of the till."

Mention of the till makes me worry. But I get some Ajax anyhow, and pretty soon Fintan has the place so you can eat off the floor. Which leads to our first tug-of-war.

"If I leave it unlocked," I explain, "every bum off the street'll be in there."

"Bums need a toilet too, Mickey," he laughs. "And if it's clean, they keep it so." He tells a story then about a café in Donegal Town that got in the papers for keeping its toilet padlocked with a chain. "Sure, we'd only have to clean it," the waitress explained, "if we left it open."

I tell him then of the café in Liverpool in October, 1955. Where I had sausage and chips at seven a.m., just off the boat from Dublin on my way to the States. Of the knives and forks chained to the table, which the waitress wiped with a rag after clearing away the empty plates. I hadn't a clue about what I would do in America. Only a phone number for Aunt Kate, my mother's sister, who was living there. In some part of Boston called Dorchester, wherever that was. Sean Hickey, from the same road in Marino, had come out with me. A moody, ginger-haired fellow, a year older, who had hung out more with my brother Jack than me. But who also wanted to try out the States at the same time that I decided to come over.

I remember we ordered our first American breakfast at this joint on Tremont Street. "How do you want your eggs?" the waitress had asked. "Sunny-side up, over light, scrambled, poached?"

"Jaysus, cooked!" Sean said, while I sat there, feeling like we'd landed on another planet. "Four toasted blues," the waitress hollered through the hatch, leaving us to puzzle what the table behind us was eating. When I asked for tea, she brought a cup with a tea bag trailing a string with a tag stapled on it. Seated there, looking at it, I had felt like crying.

"Another planet is right," Fintan tells me, and I go home that night happy to have another Irish on the job. Even one with an earring.

The rest-room door stays locked all the same. Though Fintan opens it for any derelict, most of whom, I admit, admire its tidiness. "You could clean your razor in that urinal," one wino marvels, making me wonder if I'm running a garage or hotel?

Our location in Central Square, six blocks down from City Hospital, and midway between O'Brien's Tavern and The Shamrock Inn, ensures a certain class of foot traffic at all hours. Dipsos, junkies, and loony tunes, we get them all. You see them drifting in and out of the alley next to us, which runs in behind the tenements, leading nowhere. There's a Dunkin Donuts directly across from us, however, which keeps the riffraff from congregating at the mouth of the alley. On account of there being a police cruiser usually double-parked outside, like having a cop permanently on duty. There was a bit of a flap last year, after a Boston radio station ran this contest. Asking listeners to call in and guess whether there'd be a cop or not in a particular donut shop. After which the DJ would ring up and inquire was there an officer on the premises? And, yes, most of the time, there was.

In any case we have only ever been held up once. And that was by a hood, not a wino or head-case. Sal the Italian still owned the place then, but I was the one working that afternoon, when this greaser came in wearing a black tee-shirt, one lazy eye and hair slicked back like a duck's arse. I asked him what he wanted, and he actually produced a gun — which in 1967 was a good few years before every school kid started packing one. I wasted no time handing over the day's take from the till, and that was that. I can still see the guy's face, looking almost as scared as I was, tongue working the inside of his cheek like a squirrel. It took the cops fifteen minutes to show after I rang, but that's probably on account of Dunkin Donuts across the road being only a dry cleaners then?

Dunkin Donuts was also a pizza parlour and burger joint previously, whereas this garage has been a garage since the 1930s. A drug store sits diagonally across the intersection from us, with a grey four-storey tenement the other side of Broadway, making up the fourth corner. The corner location is what keeps this place afloat. Providing the volume that allows me pay the bills out of the penny or two the multinationals let you make on a gallon of petrol. A gallon of gas, so. Christ knows, it took me long enough to stop saying bonnet for hood and boot for trunk. And Fintan's only halfway there yet. The first half, as in wind-screens for what are wind-shields here. Which makes for a few puzzled looks when he offers to clean them for punters who pull up to the pumps. On the other hand, it's from him I've learned lingo like "multinationals", as he's always giving out about big business. Like he's some kind of a Communist as well as a piece of work.

IT WAS LATE MARCH when I took Fintan on. The same week it felt like winter maybe wasn't going to last forever. There was even a bit of warmth in it, the sun having finally fired up enough to begin melting the snow in patches, as if the ground were pushing up underneath. I always forget how spring does that — pushes up from below. Crocuses and snowdrops breaking through the soil, reminding you that the bulbs have been buried there all along. Massachusetts weather is a bit Irish — you can get snow in April — but you knew that week spring was around the corner. Or if not that, only a few blocks away.

By mid-April Maggie is at me to take down the storm windows. While all I want to do is get out in the garden and start digging. I take the windows down instead, remembering when we used to nail plastic sheeting with laths to the sashes to keep the draughts out. When heating oil went sky-high in the early Seventies, however, we went into hock to have the house fitted with proper storm windows. And screens which slide into place during the warm weather, to keep the shagging mosquitoes out. I remember the first summer mosquitoes and

I were introduced. The bites swelling up the size of walnuts, which I scratched till they bled. However, I don't react to them like that anymore, the blood having thinned out, I suppose, three decades on.

The house is a small, tidy duplex down in Cambridgeport, towards the river, just off Magazine Street. We rent the ground floor, figuring the tenants get our noise over twelve months, while we get their heat winters. It's worked out OK over the years. The tenants also get to use the front porch for the good weather, while we have the garden out back. Plus the basement which has a door into it from the garden, where I have a work bench and an easy chair. Aunt Kate came over from Dorchester to live in the downstairs flat when we bought the house, the year JFK got shot. She died a couple of years later, and since then we've had five or six sets of tenants. I try to rent to young couples who I think are saving to buy their own house. Figuring they won't be blowing their money on booze and loud parties.

Right now we have this Portagee pair, Luis and Fatima Da Silva, who are about five years over from the Azores. Usually the Portagees end up in East Cambridge — though Eastie, where Sal at the garage lived, was all Italians when I first came over. Property prices have rocketed of course, but Luis and Fatima are hustlers, and I figure they'll have their down payment saved in another year or so. Both working twelve-hour shifts in a dry-cleaners, which is hotter than hell summers. And stinks something terrible even if you're just collecting a jacket, never mind working there. Every Saturday they head off early to the fruit & vegetable market in Haymarket Square, where the produce is fresher and cheaper. Like Moore Street in Dublin, I suppose. Though I doubt the North End has anyone like your woman who used to sell oranges there when I was a kid, the huge lip hanging off her like a saucer. I couldn't take my eyes off her the first time I saw her, and got a clatter from my mother for staring. These days I slag Luis, setting off with his string bags for Haymarket. "Yous are solid immigrant stock," I say, reminding him he's the first 'ethnic' I've ever rented to.

I only rented to Irish once. Jackie Callaghan, a quiet bloke from Roscommon, who pretty much kept to himself. He got taken on permanent, after a while, by the Cambridge fire department, and eventually bought a house up in Arlington. Cambridgeport, the neighbourhood where we live — or "the Port" as I eventually learned to call it — always had a scattering of Irish, or Irish-Americans. But nowhere as thick on the ground as North Cambridge, let's say, or Kerry Corner. The Port always had coloureds too, even if I hadn't that entirely sussed, when Maggie and I were buying. Though I knew Riverside, a few blocks west, was black with them, so to speak. The coloureds around us are quiet enough, but it's gotten too dangerous after dark in recent years. So much so that Maggie doesn't go out now after seven o'clock in summer, and four in wintertime.

Of course the Port's changed other ways, too. Younger couples with real money are buying in, and I'm seeing Volvos and BMWs parked between here and the Square, when I'm walking to work mornings. Maybe "real" money isn't quite right, as a lot of them are lawyers and accountants. Or brokers, who pull it in doing stuff with paper that somehow makes more money? Maybe "big" — not "real" — money is more what I mean? Anyhow, a lot of the old neighbourhood has died off, or moved on, since the early Seventies. And a lot of the Irish cleared out even earlier. Like Jackie Callaghan, downstairs, just as soon as he could afford a picket-fence pillbox up in Arlington.

It's funny, but I sometimes now use the term "Irish" to mean Irish-American. Guys whose father or grandfather came over. Whereas, when I first came over, I wouldn't have called them "Irish" in a fit. Even if that's all they ever call themselves. It's the same way as you call guys "Italians" here — who've never even visited Italy.

What's also funny is how I never palled around much with the real Irish here? Which maybe explains why I took so to Fintan at work? Sure, we all drank together in Dorchester, when I was living with Aunt Kate, but that ended after I met Maggie and moved across the Charles River to Cambridge back in 1959. There were fewer Irish here to begin with and hardly any Dubs. Those Irish I met this side of the river were all from the country. Kerry mostly, and Kerry is another country altogether. Everything's "the Kingdom" with them, and cute doesn't begin to describe the carry-on. Though I did pal with JoJo Boyle for years, in O'Brien's, till the drink caught up with him. JoJo was from Sligo, and the fact that neither of us were part of the Kerry mafia probably explains why we took up together.

Of course Sean Hickey who came over with me had stopped at Aunt Kate's for a while. And, when things seemed slow enough in Boston those first months, we had decided to try our luck that spring in Chicago. Except neither of us cared for that town, the wind off Lake Michigan enough to freeze you solid, even in April. Thumbing back to Boston a few weeks later, we ended up stranded in some one-cow town near Erie, Pennsylvania. Standing with our thumbs out for hours. And fairly starving too, as we had only fifty cents between us.

It was early days yet in America, and a lot of things still struck us as odd. Like the road sign we were standing next to:

> **Thickly**
> **35 MPH**
> **Settled**

"It's settled with thicks all right," Sean said, after the hundredth car passed by.

"Feck it," I finally decided, heading for a café across the road. We took care to take a table near the door, and I ordered everything off the menu. Eggs every-which-way, bacon, sausage, pancakes, home fries — the works. Sean's stomach was suddenly not right, however, so he just ordered a cup of coffee and a donut. He waited till I was nearly finished, then got up and went over to the cash register. "Here's what I owe you," he gave the owner thirty cents. "But you'll have to run like fuck to collect from him," he pointed over at me.

I got out the door just ahead of the owner. And when I caught up to Sean outside the town, I hurled a hundred rocks at him. Which he dodged, laughing all the while. An hour later we caught a lift in a car transporter, hauling six 1956 T-Birds to a dealer in Quincy, Massachusetts. Which left me with a soft spot for that car for years to come.

I saw less of Sean after he got work as a painter in the Boston Navy Yard in 1957, and moved out from Aunt Kate's. He was living in Southie last time I saw him, back in the Seventies, when our Lucy was around ten. It was Paddy's Day, and JoJo and I were in a bar after the parade, when Sean came in. The same shock of red hair, only that day there was also red smeared below his eye from this nasty-looking cut. "Some nigger last night," Sean spat out, "with a fistful of rings."

"You want to clean that off, Sean?" I motioned towards the toilets. But Sean just sat and ordered a beer, as if the blood were some kind of stigmata. We got fairly stuck in then, and near closing time we were pretty well smoked. Next thing I knew, Sean turned to this lad from Killarney on a stool next to him.

"Fish-hooks is what you Kerry hoors have in your pockets," Sean informed him, "when it comes your turn to buy a round." JoJo shoved Sean off his stool then, before anyone else could. And we got out of there quick before anything serious started.

I GOT IN WITH a Boston construction company after we landed back from Chicago that time. Two or three summers later, the building game went slack, but I found work at Revere Beach near the airport where I met Sal. It was the same summer I met Maggie, and the fact that she lived in Cambridge persuaded me to take the job which Sal kept offering me at his garage. Not that it all happened together, by any means.

As it was, I liked taking the subway out to Revere afternoons, where I'd walk along the beachfront before work. Sometimes I'd get an Italian ice: a paper cone full of shaved ice with a few shakes of coloured syrup out of these tall bottles. Raspberry, lemon & lime, or grape. I've seen it called "slush" elsewhere, which is accurate, but "Italian ice" sounds classier. Anyhow, you could spot the local men, most of them

Italians, by the way they stood. Braced against the promenade wall, staring up through dark glasses at the sun, which had their skin the colour of leather. "Baked potato people," Maggie used to call them. And always wearing something gold: necklace, bracelet or rings.

There was always plenty of water in Dublin, so seeing the ocean from this side made me that bit less homesick, I suppose. One summer my mother had taken my brother Jack, my sister Lizzie, and me by train to Bray, which had hobby-horses and dodgems, like Revere. And when we were a little older, Jack and I would cycle down to Dollymount Strand.

In Revere you saw what looked like the same gulls, riding the breeze over the waves. While a few old men and women sat under the pavilions above the beach, a pigeon or two overhead in the eaves. When night fell, however, it was a different scene. Souped-up hot rods and Harleys cruising the beach strip, not a muffler among them. While the lights on the games of chance and food stands looked like Christmas in the middle of summer. Plus the pizza always smelled stronger at night. An almost exotic smell back then, before there was a pizza place on every corner of America.

The guy I was working for owned the Ferris wheel along with some other rides. As well as a hot dog stand and a bar, all on the strip across from the beach. I worked them all: cooking franks, or wiping up the sick in a Ferris-wheel car where some kid had tossed his chips and candy floss. Only I was learning to say french fries and cotton candy. Then maybe the next night in the bar, I'd be pulling pints for the locals, nearly all men, and possibly one or two couples who had come down to the beach for the evening. Sal was from Revere, only he had moved to Cambridge, from where he would come back every few nights to visit his mother. Then sit at the bar and have a few pops. He never spoke, until one night he asked did I know that Christopher Columbus was a mechanic?

I shook my head, not sure I'd heard him right.

"How else you think he got 3,000 miles to the galleon?"

That was so pitiful I had to laugh, and after that night we began to chat.

Another night Sal told me how his father had landed in Revere. It seems he'd paid $500 in Sicily for the passport of a deceased Italian-American, then explained to the Immigration lads at Ellis Island, as best he could, how his parents hadn't liked the States. And so took him back with them to Italy when he was an infant, which was why he hadn't any English. His father had then got a job in a bakery in Brooklyn. And a girlfriend, another Sicilian, who had a row with him one night. Still browned off the next morning, she rang the Immigration & Naturalization Service and reported him. The INS came round to his aunt's house, where his father was living. The aunt told them she hadn't seen him in days. She rang the bakery after the Feds left, warning him not to come home. So instead of going there, Sal's father hopped a bus to Boston and got a job in a shoe factory in Revere. Fifteen years later, he was able to reclaim his real name, Enrico LoPresti, when President Roosevelt declared a general amnesty for illegal aliens.

For some reason, maybe because I was living with my aunt too, Sal took a shine to me, and kept offering me a job. Or maybe it was because I told him the odd story back. "I know fuck-all about cars," I told him one night. "It's my Uncle Derek you want." Uncle Derek, who sold used motors out of his back lane in Killester. When he wasn't travelling halfway round the world in the merchant marine. Sending back postcards from places like Galveston or Singapore, which I kept in a shoebox under my bed

"He won an old Bentley in a card game once," I told Sal one night. "The car was in mint condition, so he advertised it in an English paper. And got a phone call from this Brit, who arranged to fly into Dublin that Saturday. He showed up at the uncle's house in a suit and tie, carrying a small black valise. 'There's the keys,' Derek said. 'Take it out on the Malahide Road.' 'No need for that, sir,' said the Brit, handing the uncle back the keys. 'Would you mind starting it up?' Meanwhile the suit & tie spiv took this sawed-off length of two-by-four from his case. Some dark wood, mahogany maybe, about eighteen inches long. Putting one end of it under the bonnet, and his ear to the other, like it's a stethoscope, he moved it along the cylinder head, listening for knocks or ticks. 'Sorry, sir,' he told the uncle, 'but this isn't the one.'

"He put away his block of wood," I told Sal that night, "and caught the next flight back to London."

"It's not your Uncle I want, but the Limey with the two-by-four!" Sal had said, throwing down a quarter tip. "You're wasting yourself pumping beer, Irish, when you could be pumping gas for me in Cambridge."

I didn't meet Maggie working the bar, however. That happened another night on the Ferris wheel, where you had to distribute the weight just so. Spacing the punters out if there wasn't a full load. Only the kid who helped run it didn't always bother his arse about that. One night a rod got bent, jamming the wheel, and I had to climb clear to the top with an outsized monkey wrench. I'd noticed the two girls get on all right, a blonde and a redhead. And as luck had it, they were in the car stranded at the top. The blonde, Maggie's sister Patti it turned out, was scared to death. But Maggie was cool enough to chat me up, putting an arm around Patti who had begun to cry, while I wrestled with the banjaxed rod. It was a memorable meeting, I suppose, the coloured lights on the Ferris wheel shining off Maggie's long hair. And more lights along the honky-tonk strip below us, while across the road the ocean was lapping up on the strand. And further beyond, Boston Harbour and the airport, with even more coloured lights on the landing strip.

The repair job took me long enough to learn that Maggie was on her nightly break from selling tickets at a stall up the strip, where you shot these high-powered water guns at a line of yellow plastic ducks swimming past. It mightn't seem much of a job to travel out from Cambridge for, but Revere Beach in summer was a buzzy kind of place. Especially in 1959, when buzzy wasn't all around you, like nowadays.

I took the Blue Line with her and her sister as far as Haymarket that night. Seeing them onto the Green Line to Park Street, where they got the Red Line back to Cambridge. Nearly as many colours as there had been earlier atop the big wheel, below it, and beyond. The next night I went down to Maggie's stall on my break, where by the end of the week I was fairly knocking the ducks over as they bobbed past. If we got a break together, we sometimes walked along the water, the pop songs from the hobby horses, or carousel, as Maggie called it, trailing up the beach behind us. Her grandparents on both sides were from Ireland, Cork and Leitrim, and it felt more like we came from opposite ends of the same planet than altogether different worlds. Maggie was quiet, but sensible, not giddy like I found a lot of American girls.

She wasn't comfortable coming into the bar on her break, though, when I was working there. So to make up for those shifts, I asked could I see her any night we both had off? That happened a few times, and we arranged to meet downtown, where we went to the pictures, *Ben Hur* one time. "Can you imagine my sister Patti on that chariot ride?" Maggie laughed over her ice cream soda afterwards.

Before long it was August, and Maggie was already looking for work, once the amusements shut down for the season. My boss wanted me to work through the winter in the bar, but one night I asked Sal if the grease monkey offer was still on?

"Who said anything about letting you near grease, Irish?" Sal laughed. "Pumping gas is what I promised."

So, a week later, I got off the Red Line in Central Square, Cambridge, and crossed Mass Ave to Prospect Street, walking a few blocks down to Sal's Atlantic garage, with its big round sign with a red-winged horse. Sal showed me how to work the pumps, and the rest is, I suppose, history? After a few weeks he had me changing flat tyres, or helping him with simple tune-up, and after six months or so, I was getting as greasy as him.

"Which comes naturally to you Wops," I told him, "but's not so easy for a Paddy."

Maggie and I continued to see each other. Only it was easier then, because I was off work in her home town every night by six o'clock. I began to call round once a week or so to her house, a few blocks over from the garage, just behind Saint Mary's. Where I got to meet the grandfather from Leitrim, who lived with them. A quiet old man in a cap in the corner of the sitting room, who wanted to talk about putting down spuds and saving turf. We were both Irish, but it was like he was from another country altogether, and I was always happy when Maggie was ready to go out. Bowling sometimes at the alley just off Essex Street, though she had to teach me how, while I tried to show her how to shoot pool at the tables there. And at least every second week to the pictures.

It was still more like we were friends than anything else, but by the next summer we were agreed it was fairly serious, so we began to save in earnest. Three years later we made the down payment on the house in the Port, which we used to pass, walking down to the river. And three months after that we got married in Saint Mary's. With Maggie's sister Patti, from atop the Ferris wheel, as maid of honour and JoJo Boyle from Sligo, and O'Brien's Tavern, as my best man. And the rest is — together with the daughter Lucy, who came along the following year — more history, I suppose?

NEARLY TWENTY-FIVE years later, and Maggie and I still live in that same house. And I still walk to work each morning, up from the Port and across Mass Ave and down Prospect to the garage. Central Square has been left to run down the last few years, which usually means the developers can't be far behind, only this time I think they have gone bust, too. The ice cream parlour which replaced Garrity's Egg & Milk shop on the corner of Norfolk Street closed up overnight, a For Rent sign in its window. Maggie had stopped buying eggs there shortly after we married, complaining that Garrity was always giving her the eye.

"Can you blame him?" I used to tease her, but there was something gamey about him all right. Freckled yellowy skin like a lizard, and buggy eyes that bulged whether he was mentally undressing a lady customer or not. A dirty old man, though he wasn't even that old yet. Dirty old man or *viejo verde*, which along with a few curses, is all the Spanish I learned from Rafael who worked for me in the garage some years ago. Who said that it translated something like an "old green smarm". Only a yellow smarm, I suppose, in Garrity the eggman's case? Like I said already, I never hired a PR or Puerto Rican. Instead, Rafael was from the Dominican Republic. Which I looked up in Lucy's school atlas at home. His crowd aren't called DRs, either. Probably because there aren't as many about as the Puerto Ricans. *Mañana* was another word I learned from Rafael, mostly because it was always *mañana* he was going to finish a job, which is why he only lasted a year at the garage. Of course sacking him ended the Spanish lessons. Which seemed a bit of a shame, seeing as I had by then fairly learned how to speak American.

Anyhow, the Port is still lovely to walk to work through in spring, all these years on. The forsythia coming on, or the maple pollen, floating like gold dust on puddles in the road after it rains. And later, tiny maple seedlings springing up where the sidewalk has cracked. Last week I passed this old fellow, a right Mr Clean & Tidy, trying to rake up magnolia petals from the footpath outside his house. There are even some elms left along Western Ave, that somehow escaped the Dutch elm disease. Great lofty trees under which these three tall skinny coloured guys sit in lawn chairs each morning early.

"Rice farmers from Haiti," Fintan informs me when I remark on them. Haiti being the other half of the Dominican Republic, according to Lucy's old atlas. Though who can keep up with the names changing on half the countries every year?

"One of those lads now runs the numbers for the Haitians," Fintan adds, however he knows this stuff. He plays the numbers himself of course, sometimes taking down a license plate off a car at the pumps, and he plays the lottery scratch-cards too. But how he knows who's running the numbers for the frigging Haitians is what stumps me?

By early May the maples are in leaf, and I've the vegetable beds dug, ready for planting. The weather is warmer too, enough so you can sometimes tell by four o'clock which candy they're making at the NECCO factory a few blocks east down Mass Ave. Caramel or chocolate, if the wind is blowing right. It makes the walk that bit sweeter the odd afternoon I knock off early to go home and garden. But it's sweetened also by the fact that I can leave Fintan in charge of the garage — and the Greek kid Evangelis — with an easy mind. Fintan told me they put him on the till at the Donegal Town garage where he first worked, before going over to London in his early twenties. I left Dublin myself around that age, though at fifty-nine I must have about twenty-five years on him? Still, I walk anywhere I can, which keeps the weight down. Plus I've my own teeth and hair yet, though the latter has maybe three black strands left among the grey.

I doubt many people had cars down the country, places like Donegal, when I left Ireland. Other than the priests and the bank managers maybe. But it so happens that Fintan is an ace mechanic. He even troubleshoots the electronics in the newer models which I don't like. High-energy ignitions, pick-up coils and control modules, like stuff out of Star Trek. "People nowadays are driving appliances," I tell Fintan. "Toasters, not cars."

"So you better learn to fix toasters, Mickey?" he says, which is hard to argue with. What's more, one of those

ComputerTune joints opened up last year, a few blocks further north down Prospect, towards the Somerville line. So far I haven't seen a drop in the number of tune-ups we do, but I wasn't especially pleased to see that crowd set up shop just down the road, either. It's a rip-off, of course. You drive into the repair bay, where they've this huge computer suspended from the ceiling, and they slip this hose from the computer over your exhaust pipe. Like it's giving your car a blow job, says Evangelis, which is the first clever thing I've heard him say. The computer then spits out this sheet of paper. Like the report cards Lucy got in primary school, saying your carburetor's scoring only 70%, or at 62% your ignition wires are in danger of failing math. The "technician", if you don't mind, then changes your air filter and replaces your plugs, same as a mere mechanic would. So why pay for a blow-job, when it's a hand-job you need? Which is the second clever thing ever from Evangelis, who'd clearly had his Wheaties that morning. ComputerTune does all this for $49.95, which is an attractive price. But Fintan, who worked for them in Florida, says they try to load on more extras than a Chinese take-away.

"Florida was sweet all right," Fintan says when I ask him. "A few of us had this cottage a few miles out of Gainesville. Right on a lake where the sun used to come up mornings like a big red ball."

"You swim in the lake?" Evangelis wants to know. Which surprises me, as I thought kung fu was the only exercise in his curriculum. That very morning he'd been moaning about how stupid the Chinese were. For not knowing it was the Greeks who invented karate. "Along with the rest of Western civilisation," I point out, which only encourages him. Making me think there must be a "Thickly Settled" sign outside his house for sure.

"I used to swim mornings," Fintan says, "before going into work. But not at night on account of the gators."

Evangelis looks interested, so Fintan, who's a fund of facts, explains how alligators are nocturnal feeders. Coming into the lake at night from the surrounding swamp, looking for fish, plus raccoon and possums along the shore. At dawn they go back into the swamps. I listen a bit myself, as Maggie loves this kind of wildlife stuff, and it might give us something to talk about.

"They're inquisitive," Fintan tells E-Man, "so splashing around at night only invites trouble. And fast enough on land that you better be able to go from zero to sixty in ten seconds yourself."

"Vroooom, vroooom," laughs Evangelis, before I send him out to help some lady unlock her gas cap. We're up to our own arses in alligators then, over the next couple of hours, both bays full and a steady stream of punters at the pumps.

The computerised tune-ups in Florida were a drag, however, according to Fintan. Most customers only wanted a tune-up, and you rarely got to track down any problem that had a client stumped. Which is the kind of diagnostic stuff, I know myself, that keeps you interested, midst all the mickey-mousing around, the punctures, or just pumping gas. The trick, of course, is to solve the puzzle for the punter. And then, if you're really smart, reveal it. Let's say some bozo drives in, panicking because every time he takes his foot off the gas, his car cuts out. Which has never happened before, so now he's worrying whether his car's just shit the bed?

If you're lucky, all that's wrong is his PCV hose has popped off, creating a vacuum leak which sucks too much air into the engine, so it cuts out. Or maybe the EGR valve is stuck open, which would likewise cause a car to stall. The trick is simply to pop the hose back on. Or give the top of the valve a tap with a wrench to unstick it. Then you explain the problem to the owner, in so much as he can follow it. And charge him a couple of bucks for the labour. Chances are the guy will be so stunned at your integrity, at his luck in finally locating an honest mechanic midst a sea of sharks, that you'll have a customer for life. Or at least for a return visit, in which you don't zap him either. Which is how I've built up what steady custom I have, and I make sure anybody working for me operates that way, too. Fintan was like that already, which makes it easy, while Evangelis is too thick to seriously fiddle a customer.

Fintan's good with the customers all right, especially like I said, the non-paying kind. A couple of older dipsos en route to the City Hospital detox floor now regularly stop by to sing *Danny Boy* or *Kevin Barry* for us. One of them, Maguire, I knew years ago from O'Brien's, before he got permanently barred. For sweeping a stack of glasses into the ice trough behind the bar one night. After the cops haul him off, Barney O'Sullivan, another regular, gets up on a chair and sticks a piece of black tape across Maguire's face in the photograph of the O'Brien's Tavern softball team, hung above the bar. Maguire looks a free agent now all right: unshaven, a scab on his chin. While his mate is an even nastier-looking article, tall and skinny, his jacket open over a dirty tee-shirt. One day he asks Evangelis where the young girls hang out? And does he know any whores?

"There's money to be made in pimping, boy," he tells E-Man.

"Fuck you," replies Evangelis.

For a moment I wonder is the tall fellow going to mix it up with Athens' answer to Bruce Lee? But E-Man is nineteen years young, built like a brick shit-house, and the pair of lushes finally do fuck off down the alley next to us.

One afternoon we're treated to the same verse of *Galway Bay* about a dozen times by another of our new Irish pals. Fintan eventually gives him a dollar just to go away.

"Saint Mary's is two blocks over," I tell Fintan, "if you want to lead a choir."

"My mother used to write 'Do you ever miss Mass, son?'" Fintan tells me at the mention of Saint Mary's. "Truth is," he laughs, "I don't miss it a bit!"

"The Pope's saying his prayers," I tell Fintan. "Oh, Lord, will there ever be women clergy?" "Not in your lifetime, John Paul," answers God. "Oh, Lord, will the Church ever approve birth control?" "Not in your lifetime, John Paul," God replies. "Oh, Lord, will there ever be another Polish Pope?" "Not in *my* lifetime, John Paul!"

Word travels of course, and soon we are a port of call for any number of tramp steamers, half of them under an Irish flag. Before long Fintan has names for most: the Philosopher is this skinny alkie who's always staring into space, as if the price of a bottle of Ripple is floating out there in the cosmos. Though he manages to touch down long enough to check the coin return in the corner phonebooth a couple of times a day. Mario Andretti is this crippled Vietnam vet in a wheelchair, an Italian-American, who motors along by shuffling his feet on the road. My favourite is Father Flanagan, a bum with a dirty clerical collar and Cork accent, who makes out he is collecting for some charity. Fintan gives him a buck and the

31

next day he's back, mumbling the same pitch. His nicotine-stained fingers the colour of rawhide, and his hands shaking. "Father, I gave yesterday!" Fintan protests. "Oh yes, thanks very much, God Bless," the padre mutters, shuffling off. Four feathers, how are ye!

"They're like stray cats," I tell Fintan. "Feed 'em, and twenty-four hours later they're back."

"Cats eat too," responds Fintan. Still it beats television all to hell, like the afternoon this floozy and her boyfriend stagger past the garage, thumbing a lift. Amazingly a car stops, only to have your woman pass out spread-eagled on the hood, her pal doing a drunken stumble-dance beside her. The driver blows his horn, then shouts out the window, "If you want a ride, get off the fucking hood!" Another time Mario Andretti overturns his wheelchair out front. "Hold on," Fintan stops Evangelis from going to his rescue. "He'll get attention now," Fintan says, "plus money." Sure enough, a couple of pedestrians give him both.

I wouldn't wonder if Fintan takes an occasional dollar from the till for a hand-out. But I figure what Fintan borrows is only what I'd be putting in the collection basket, were I bothering with Mass anymore. Which I'm not, now Lucy's grown. Maggie still goes of course, but she's given up trying to drag me along. I draw the line, however, at leaving our loaner in the vacant lot unlocked, should one of Fintan's Apostles need a place to kip at night. He says in Donegal they often found somebody asleep in their loaner, who hadn't made it home from the pub. "At least they *had* homes to go to," I point out to Fintan.

As it is, we do an occasional tune-up for this guy with some kind of muscular ailment, who actually lives in his 1970

Plymouth. The car is a rat's nest of tins, newspapers and blankets, reeking of piss, and I can't get near it. But it doesn't take a feather out of Fintan, who's a rare bird all right, the way he can talk to anybody. "I don't have an address," the guy says when Fintan goes to write up a bill. "How about Plymouth Inn?" Fintan cracks, while I just shake my head. He pushes it with the punters, no doubt, but he gets away with it. Like this guy in a burgundy Catalina, who tells us that his doctor says he needs a heart operation, if he wants to see next Christmas.

"What's the warranty?" he asks, once we've hit him for new brakes shoes.

"Normally 6,000 miles," Fintan cracks. "But I'll give you six months instead!"

IT'S NICE HAVING another Irish around, like I said, somebody who reminds you just how different the States are. "You could live on what's thrown out over here," Fintan says, and he's got that right. Nearly thirty years here and I'm still amazed at what people discard. Trash day is best, with seventy-dollar shoes or freshly ironed trousers in rubbish bins at the kerb. Fintan has fairly furnished the room he's rented that way, over on Norfolk Street, just behind the bowling alley, and I ask him to look out for storm windows, for the small greenhouse I'm building at home.

The day I offer him an old TV I have up in the attic, however, he practically goes spare. "It's that yoke has this country fucked!" he informs me. "Plastic flowers growing out of toilets with blue water." I can more or less follow that bit, as Maggie buys the blue stuff for the hoppers at home. Though she wouldn't have a plastic flower anywhere. But I can't get my head entirely around how television has eradicated the story-telling impulse of tribes and villages? Or something to that effect?

"I take it you don't want the TV, so?" I cut him off.

Grinning, he tells me of his aunt in Donegal who, when the telly first came in, thought it bad manners for anybody to get up and walk out "on the nice young man reading the news". And then about three old bachelors in the same Donegal village, watching a programme when the electricity fails. "Where do you suppose they are?" one of the men finally asked, gesturing toward the blank screen. "Sure, sitting there in the dark," the brother answered, "same as ourselves!"

Fintan gets going on Hollywood next. Claiming twin beds were invented by the studios, who didn't want to show a married couple played by, let's say, Rock Hudson and Doris Day, in the same bed. Lest it suggest they might be, when the lights went out, actually screwing each other.

"Not that Rock Hudson ever screwed anybody in a skirt," I say. "Whatever about Doris Day."

"Right you are," says Fintan. "But Hollywood didn't want you knowing Rock was bent, either. Not when they'd just gotten most of America into twin beds." And off he goes again: about American puritanism, homosexuality, and how a fear of the body is actually a fear of death. I don't know where he comes up with half this stuff, and it takes me another week to figure out he's not bent himself. Never mind the poetry, which he quotes from time to time. Still, listening to him beats listening to Evangelis, ol' Fists of Fury himself, rabbiting on about some chop-suey Western he got out on video the night before.

"What drives me spare," Fintan says another day, "is how people here insist on happiness?"

"Have a nice day!" I jeer, but he has the bit in his mouth by now.

"Happiness is but the premature profit on imminent pain," he quotes some poet, whatever that fellow was sniffing.

"You should garden," I tell him, but Fintan says he coped enough spuds growing up in Donegal to last a lifetime.

AT HOME I HAVE the flower beds looking good. The daffodils are nearly finished, but the hyacinths are only coming on. I used to deadhead the daffs, until I noticed half of them weren't blooming the next spring. I read later in a gardening book you're meant to let them wither on the stalk. So that the goodness goes back into the bulb. Kind of like letting your pint of stout settle before you drink it, I suppose. Roses you can lop straight away, of course, once the bloom is off them. Though I'm not that pushed about roses, which have a kind of snobbery attached to them, like breeding poodles. Or comparing the bouquet of this wine to the body of that — whereas the buzz is all that matters? Still, we've a lovely wild rose, from a cutting that Maggie got me to take from Crane's Beach up in Ipswich the year Lucy was born.

Meanwhile the lilac we planted by the back steps in 1963 when we bought the house is once again heavy with flowers. The lavender variety, not the newer magenta that's more popular now. It's not a huge back garden, maybe 25' x 45', but it's an entire park compared to the postage-stamp patch we had in Dublin. Most of which was taken up by the coal bunker and clothesline. Plus the shed where my father kept his birds. Our mother would run my brother Jack and I, if we tried to kick a football in it. But what I remember most is the way the snails came out from under the hedge whenever it first began to rain. And the crunching underfoot if you walked out back at night. It was too small to plant anything, beyond a few flowers in the border, which my mother tended every year.

Not that size is the answer to everything, of course. Family-size corn flakes, king-size bed, giant screen TV — everything better because it's bigger over here. Fintan claims it has to do with the wide open spaces — that America is a horizontal place, spreading out. Whereas Ireland, which is about time and history, is a vertical place, going down and back into itself.

"Latitude versus depth," he says, not that I follow his gist. Still, he has me thinking more about the States than I have in a long time. And thinking more about Ireland since I quit drinking in O'Brien's five or six years ago. Where I had gotten tired of the same old bullshit year after year, whether Kerry would get through to the All-Ireland, and so on. There wasn't any satellite feed yet, either, so you couldn't even watch the match. Though I'd lost any interest in the GAA by then. It was like Ireland itself had begun to make less and less sense anyhow? Like the fellow passing a white plastic bucket around O'Brien's for the IRA — which you felt you no longer knew much about, and the boyo with the bucket even less. Or reading the *Irish Echo* every week, which had F-all in it, apart from photos of lads as old as yourself, getting pissed at the annual Mayo Men's Association do in New York or Philly.

My mate JoJo Boyle from Sligo was also going down the tubes back then — which is probably most of the reason I stopped calling in. He'd had a tit job with the MBTA for years, selling tokens from a booth at the Central Square subway station. Only that kind of a routine would drive me demented, and it obviously hadn't done him any good. Anyhow, by 1979 JoJo was on some kind of extended sick leave, which he was spending in the third booth across from the bar in O'Brien's. His back propped against the wall, wearing the same black cardie over a stained shirt. Plus his grey MBTA trousers with the blue stripe, and his feet in an old pair of black runners sticking out of the booth

"How's Mickey," he'd say, whenever I slid into the green leather seat opposite him. Telling me then some story about Sligo that I'd heard ten times before. Until one Saturday I noticed for the first time how his nose had begun to slide sideways across his face. And the little red veins sloping off it, like secondary roads on a map. Only these were broken off, leading nowhere. Coming in that day, I had already eyed a dark stain on the redbrick front of the tavern. Where JoJo had gone to piss, the front door being that few steps nearer than the toilet at the back. O'Brien would have barred JoJo for a week, had he eyed that himself. Though I had also seen O'Brien leaning over JoJo at closing time, rubbing an ice-cube over his cheek, before getting another regular to run him home.

I had bought JoJo a highball of OT & ginger that afternoon. Then left for home, stopping in at The Buffet on the way for another beer. Which is where I've drunk ever since, if I bother going into a bar. Nothing Irish, or Irish-American, about the Buffet. And if there's no crack there, there's no sham-shamrock "Kiss me, I'm Irish" bullshit, either, especially around Paddy's Day.

I haven't been back to Ireland either, since I stopped drinking in O'Brien's. Maggie and I went over a couple of times after we were married. Hired a car and did the Ring of Kerry, if only so I could see what had the crowd from the Kingdom so enthralled. It was all right to look at, but you wouldn't grow anything on that soil. Which explains, I guess, why they are all over here. We'd stay in the home place in Dublin with my sister, Lizzie, and her family, but that was never easy. Too crowded, and too strained also. As if we were putting them out, which I suppose we were.

We stayed in a Bed & Breakfast in Drumcondra the last time we both went over, and Maggie was as happy as I not to be stopping in Marino. Like most Yanks, she's mad about Ireland. Though she's not like the worst of them, who think it's pigs in every parlour. Still, she can't stop talking about how green it is, which is a bit rich, seeing I can't shift her out of the house here. To go for a walk, or even a drive, especially since Lucy's moved out. Still, she's been over twice to Ireland with her sister Patti since I last went back. Which is the kind of compromise that marriage turns into — or at least ours has — over the years.

Certainly there's not much in Dublin that would spur me to make the trip. Both the parents are gone now. Plus half the time Lizzie and Jack aren't talking, and while I'm still on speaking terms with both, I've little to say to either. Sal and I used to talk about that at the garage years ago. Puzzling how you could grow up to find your siblings at such a distance from you. More like strangers, than people you'd played with, fought with, or even shared a bed with. Though Maggie and Patti get on well. Anyhow, Sal claimed it was more an Irish than an Italian thing. But we were always going back and forth about those differences. A lot of Italians used to come in to the garage back then, and the big thing with them about the Irish was the drink. After a while, I learned to give it back as good as I got it.

"You'll never find a Guinea drinking, when he could be eating," I'd tell Frankie, Sal's brother. "Or eating when he could be listening to opera."

"Or a Harp screwing," Frankie would shoot back, "when he could be drinking." Frankie, who had a barber shop on Columbia Street, was even easier-going than Sal. A sharp dresser too, like a lot of Italians. Always a knife-like crease to his trousers, expensive lemon polo shirts, and patent leather shit-kickers for shoes.

Italians are different about clothes, and different about family also. Closer-knit, seeing more of one another, and doing stuff — especially eating — together. It's not that they don't row with their brothers or sisters, aunts or uncles. But it's not the at-arms-length Cold War the Irish tend to conduct with their relations. More in-close fighting, that maybe estranges them less, after the blood dries and the dust finally settles? Sal claimed Italians don't trust politicians like the Irish do, because they don't trust anybody much outside of family. He knew a thing or two, Sal, and we'd chat a lot whenever it was slow. He and his crowd were Catholics too, of course, but they didn't seem so hung up by the Church somehow. I remember Frankie and he used to talk about sex like it were golf or something. "But then you won't find a Mick fucking," Frankie would tell me, "if he could be fighting."

STILL THE ONLY FIGHTING I do anymore is the odd sniping at home with the wife. And even there we're not using live ammunition most of the time. I know Maggie is missing Lucy, who got a job working with computers in California, and moved out there last year. I figure it must be missing Lucy, because she's been missing me for a good few years. As if the marriage somehow ran out of steam a while back. I don't know we even noticed it happening, though I spent a couple of years trying to get Maggie to take an interest in the garden. She's a whiz with potted plants indoors, geraniums, begonias, azaleas, but she can't be bothered trying to grow anything outside. Which is why her nature programmes on the box make me laugh. Reminding me of the time we went fishing in Boston Harbour, off a pier behind South Station, when we were courting. Maggie hooked something, a shoe or maybe even a fish. Only we never got to see because she screamed and flung the rod into the water. "I don't like eating with my hands," she declares if I suggest taking a picnic up to Crane's Beach. Like we used to do when Lucy was little, and Maggie had no problem eating out of her hands.

So we just keep ticking over down in the Port, which is largely OK with me. I still find this a beautiful town, especially this time of year. Take the other evening, for example, as I'm heading home. All these dark purple clouds behind me as I come down Prospect, past this apartment where some Puerto Rican is playing the drums. Yet the redbrick storefronts on Mass Ave, when I reach the Square, are flooded by sunlight, which bounces off a second-storey window above Libby's Liquors like it's on fire. The same sun also shines like a floodlight on this stucco house farther down Magazine Street. The same house that always catches my eye, its two tiny windows set on the Kildare side. And some creeper, which I've yet to identify, climbing the stucco wall, only this evening it looks like the shadow of a tree thrown against the wall.

Maggie seems happy enough with the house still. Though I suppose the done thing would be to have moved ourselves out to Arlington by now. I wouldn't shift there in a fit, however, even if there are no coloureds. Too many ranch houses, for openers, which remind me of boxcars. And lawns everywhere, instead of real gardens, giving you too much shagging grass to mow. You need walls or fences or hedges around you for a proper garden. Even if that means the neighbours are on top of you, like here in the Port. You can't walk anywhere in a suburb like Arlington, either; there's none of the give-and-take of city streets. Nor any interesting buildings to look at. Since you'd be bored silly walking around the neighbourhood, you end up taking the car somewhere scenic to walk, like Spy Pond further up Route 2. While here in the Port you can just walk down Magazine Street to the Charles for something scenic. Or back up to the Square and down Mass Ave, past MIT, to loop along the river to the bottom of Magazine and back home, if you're looking for a good walk. You end up living your life in a car in places like Arlington, even just to get a quart of milk. And I've spent enough of my life working on cars, so as not to want to spend my time off behind the fecking wheel. "You're off on your walkabout?" Maggie says when she sees me heading out. Walkabout being aborigine for taking a stroll, or so she says.

It seems more and more that's what people do here — buy a nice house, but never stay home. Always jumping into the car and driving off. Instead of taking a lawn chair and beer outdoors, and enjoying themselves. And even most of those staying home don't know how to relax. "They get a pair of

Bermuda shorts, a Shepherd dog, an extension ladder, and an outdoor grill," Sal used to say. "Like they're pioneers or Buffalo Bill. Next thing you know, here's one of 'em falling out of a tree, or walking around with an arm in a sling."

Still, Jackie Callaghan, who lived downstairs, didn't go native when he moved out to Arlington. If anything, he seemed even more depressed, the time he invited Maggie and me out for a few beers and a hot dog. Like he was living one of those "lives of quiet desperation" that Fintan is always rabbiting on about. Quoting some old hippie who lived in the woods further up Route 2.

SUMMER

JULY comes, and if you can smell the ripe garbage in the alleys, at least there's sun in summer, unlike bloody Ireland. The sumac trees throw their saw-toothed shadows on the sidewalk, while at home the cat Guzzles crouches on a chair by the kitchen window, waiting for a breeze. It's early July that Lionel gets hired, thanks to Fintan, I might add. A few coloured customers have always come in, but not many — which, I'll admit, suited me just fine. A carload of them might pull in for a fill-up first thing in the morning, after cruising all night. Cadillacs mostly. One time they didn't even get out during a tune-up either. Just sat in this maroon 1981 Fleetwood, passing around a beer and a joint.

Anyhow, Fintan had been mentioning this coloured mechanic he knows. How hiring him would be good for business, given our location. It happens I need to take on somebody, because Evangelis is driving me crazy, but I can't see hiring a coloured. Or 'black' as Fintan — who'd teach his grandmother to suck eggs — keeps informing me. Only I doubt his granny would tell him to fuck off, which is what I do.

"Calling them *coloured* is like the Brits calling us *Paddy*," he says.

"Horseshit," I reply. "Calling them *Roscoe* would be like calling us *Paddy*."

I have him there, too. Which doesn't happen often, seeing he's read a ton of stuff for a journeyman mechanic. "*Coloured* is simply describing them," I sum up. The daughter, Lucy, who went to school with them, stopped me from saying *nigger* years ago. But what matters is how you live your life, not what you're called. Nor am I going to hire somebody Fintan met in a coloured bar on Mass Ave, which I think he's nuts even to be drinking in.

Then two things happen. First Evangelis loses it altogether. After mooning for a month over a girl who once "admired" him, but now "admires" his older brother. I have to admit I like the way he uses "admire". Even if it's because his English isn't great, there's something mannerly to it. Quaint almost, coming from an unshaven hulk whose mother, it seems, still beats him twice a week. Anyhow, the morning after his brother gets engaged, E-Man comes stumbling out the back room, blood streaming down his noggin into his eyes. Fintan sits him down and asks him what happened. E-Man says nothing for a while. Before admitting he tried to split the back-room bench with his head.

"You must sees your head," he says, "passing through the wood." Describing the technique from some kung-fu magazine he can barely read.

"And you think the Chinese are stupid?" I tell him, as Fintan tries to wash the blood off his face. I send him home, with a whopping headache. Tell him to take a couple of days off. The next night I call around to his house with two weeks' severance pay. I tell his mother he's wasted in such a job, hoping she won't beat seven kinds of shite out of him once I leave.

The second thing happens the following night. After Luis, our tenant downstairs, offers me a beer on the front porch, where he's trying to beat the heat. We're sitting there, shooting the breeze, when Luis goes inside and comes out with a bunch of photographs. Of the Azores where he grew up, and of Angola where his family moved when he was around eight. The Azores are as green as Ireland, only a lot more vegetation. But it's one of the African photographs that stops me cold. It's this black and white snapshot of Luis and his younger brother, standing either side of their father, who is smiling at the camera. While each of his sons holds the severed head of a coloured Angolan. By the hair, like they were some kind of a trophy fish or a couple of pheasants. Luis doesn't pass any comment on it, beyond explaining there was a kind of a war on.

I don't ask any questions either. But I can't get the picture out of my head. Even in the garden, watering the tomatoes once the sun is off them, so the roots won't scorch. It pops up again when I go to bed that night, too. The fact it was a snapshot makes it worse somehow. Like something from a family album, instead of a newspaper or on TV, where you can expect to see anything. Too hot to sleep, I lie there thinking of it. And of Sean Hickey from our road in Marino, only as I last saw him in that Southie bar on Paddy's Day, his face bloodied by a nigger with a fistful of rings.

And, because that's the way my mind's going, I suddenly remember this other photo. In the *Boston Globe* about ten years ago, of this anti-busing demonstration outside Boston City Hall. A photo of this coloured guy getting whacked in the face with the staff of this huge American flag some white kid is carrying. I thought it was absolutely criminal they were busing coloureds to school in Southie back then. But there was something wrong about that newspaper photo too? The coloured fellow minding his own business, walking to work in a suit and tie. Which is not the story, of course, with the young bloods you cross the street to avoid nowadays. In my heart I know the difference between coloureds and us is clear-cut. Black and white if you like. And I never pay Fintan much heed, going on about colonial this and imperialist that. But lying there, listening to this mosquito overhead, I can't help thinking the photo of those two coloureds — or their heads rather, eyes open for the camera — is wrong. Wrong in the way all the stuff we learned in school about the Brits — the penal laws and the famine — is wrong.

Or was Luis' father giving his sons those heads to hold what is really wrong? I can't puzzle that out at all. My father may never have bothered his arse much about us. But I can't imagine him setting up that kind of snap for the family album, either. I start wondering next where Sean Hickey ended up, until Maggie tells me she can't sleep with my tossing and turning.

"We should get twin beds, so," I tell her, "like Rock Hudson and Doris Day." But I get up finally, and go out to the sofa in the sitting room. Hoping in vain for a bit of a breeze from the three windows onto the street.

I mention the photo Luis showed me to Fintan at work the next morning. Who quotes more poetry at me: "Those who have evil done to them, do evil in return." I'm not clear what evil was done to the Da Silvas in Africa. But by then this old DeSoto has pulled in, trailing enough white smoke to elect a Pope, so I don't bother asking either.

The DeSoto's head gasket is fucked, just like I thought. To replace it would cost more than the car's worth, however, so I level with the owner. A Korean, who has just enough English to understand his car has bought the farm. He seems interested in a 1970 VW bug I have for sale in the garage yard, however. So I tell him to think it over and come back tomorrow, as there is another party also interested in it. Though I don't tell the Korean it's a secondhand VW dealer, at the Old Volks Home over on Hampshire Street, who only wants it for parts.

I don't think any more about the photo that morning, but the next day I tell Fintan I've sacked Evangelis.

"You mean benched him, Mickey," laughs Fintan, who's mad for American baseball.

Fintan then takes his time on a couple of punctures, leaving me to run back and forth to the pumps like a blue-arsed fly. Just in case I haven't yet twigged we are now shorthanded. Around noon, then, Fintan mentions Lionel again. "So have your pal come in," I surprise both of us. "And we'll talk about part-time for openers."

Lionel comes in that afternoon. Which suggests he's hungry for a job, never a bad sign. The first thing I notice are two diamond studs in his left ear. Explaining, no doubt, why he and Fintan are such soul mates. I have him fill out an application first. I only bother with applications to have an address, after one bastard I hired did a runner with two-hundred dollars' worth of wrenches. We chat for a minute or two in the office with its old magazines. And its coffee machine for any customers too cheap to go across to Dunkin Donuts for a decent cup, while waiting on their car. On the wall is this old sign: NO $10 BILLS BEFORE NOON PLEASE. Sal thought it real funny, and I've never taken it down. Though we'd be in trouble if we didn't see a ganseyload of tenners nowadays by noon.

Lionel, who looks like an ageing middleweight, shaved head and all, doesn't touch his coffee, which shows some taste. Somewhere in his forties, he looks fit, with a light step and long, ropey arms. Still, I'm not easy talking to him. Coloureds make me nervous at best, and I'm feeling browned off at Fintan for having talked me into this.

Lionel, meanwhile, looks me straight in the eye. Which should settle me, only I've known a couple of con-men along the way who made a real point of doing that, too. He tells me he was twenty years in the Army, a motor pool mechanic, including Vietnam.

"We don't do many oil changes on tanks in here," I tell him.

"Won't be long," he laughs, "way this neighbourhood's going."

"We also worked on jeeps and staff cars," he adds. "Along with the big stuff."

Anyhow, I tell him he can start at noon the next day. He shows up fifteen minutes early and does some hand-slapping jive with Fintan. Which they must teach them early in Donegal? I plan to use him on repairs, as I don't want to risk losing any of my regular gas customers, who might be put off by a coloured. Lionel is all kinds of willing, however. And quick too, so that by six that evening I'm worn out trying to beat him to the pumps.

He knows what I'm up to, also, and I'm not happy with that. Even if it's only this look he gives me the following day, after I cut in front of him to fill up Mrs Casey's old Chevy. "Yes, indeed," he says, making this little bow, arms spread wide, before walking back to the garage. He doesn't say anything more. But it's like he has the upper hand now, which unsettles me. I go over all the same, to look at the fan belt he's replacing on a Buick Rivera.

"You got that socket wrench?" he gives me this level look.

"You got no brains, you gotta have feet," I say, shuffling off to retrieve it at the pumps where I'd thrown it down. "Fuck this for a game of Indians," I tell myself coming back. Fed up with being flustered when I'm supposed to be boss of the works.

The Buick is the kind of mickey-mouse task I start somebody new off on. Especially as I'm not sure personnel carriers or rocket launchers even have fan belts. Lionel has the job done already, however, the belt nice and tight. Evangelis was so slow you could time him with a calendar, but Lionel looks to be as quick as Fintan, who has proved no slouch.

He keeps pumping gas, too, where I notice he's friendly with the punters in a kind of a quiet way. Unless it's another coloured, like the guy in a beige Bonneville yesterday. Big bush of hair on him, like they all wore years ago.

"Say what?" goes Lionel.

"Chicken butt!" says the other guy. Which must be coloured talk for ten gallons and check the oil?

"You're talking from behind your ears," he tells another black customer a few hours later. "You ain't smart. Nor good lookin'."

Some days he comes in wearing a clean sky-blue vest, which shows off this Chinese dragon tattooed on his bicep. The tatoo, together with shaved head and earrings, makes him look like a frigging pirate. All of which I figure might be a bit much for the Mrs Caseys I've courted down the years. So even as I'm throwing in the towel about him pumping gas, I have to ask him to wear something with sleeves.

"No problem," he says. "But can you dig it?" Flexing his arm so that the dragon's eyes widen slightly. "Got that done in Thailand. On R & R."

"I could use some Rest & Relaxation myself," I reply.

I notice he wears some kind of perfume too, which I ask Fintan about.

"Coconut oil."

"Perfume?"

"So is after-shave," shrugs Fintan. Who mentions later that gorse in Donegal gives off a scent like coconut on a warm spring day. Plants I can figure out, so I ask Fintan about gorse and whins. And heather, which Maggie once tried to grow in a pot indoors.

"You can start full-time next week," I tell Lionel a few days later, "provided you work Saturdays."

"Right on, Boss," he says. He calls me "Boss" a lot. And Fintan "Irish", like Sal used to call me. I'm still wary round him, but he looks good under the hood. And he's not yet fiddling the till, far as I can gauge.

I give him Larry Ferguson's Dodge a few days later. In for its third clutch in four years. Larry's nearly eighty, deaf as a post, but motoring still.

"You'd do better buying him a hearing aid," Lionel says, after he has the job done.

"How's that?" I ask. Wondering is he being smart about Larry? Even if Larry had to be told three times what he owed.

"Dude can't hear when he oughta let the clutch out," Lionel explains. "That's how come he's burning them out."

It makes sense, all right. And I have to admit I'm impressed, not having sussed that myself. Along with never having figured Larry Ferguson for a dude before.

I notice Lionel also tries to explain stuff to women customers, something I rarely do. "It's only flat on the bottom," I might point out to a lady who comes in with a puncture. To see can I catch her out. But Lionel actually shows them the nail or stone that has caused the flat. When the lady who owned the Buick Rivera came back that afternoon, I heard him telling her how fan belts don't grip as much, ever since they started putting more nylon than rubber in them.

"You're wasting your breath," I tell him as the Buick drives off.

"Uh, uh," he says. "Women know about nylon." He tells then how his fan belt broke when he and his Diane were courting. "I asked for her pantyhose," Lionel laughs, "which jus' about got us back to her house."

"I bet she carried a spare fan belt in her purse after that," says Fintan. "You smooth-talking devil, you."

"Or a spare pair of pantyhose," I want to say, only I'm too tense around Lionel. And even more uptight when Fintan runs his mouth like that, as if I'm not sure how a coloured guy is going to take it? Though I notice Lionel doesn't take it any differently. Just smiles and throws a screwdriver at Fintan, who skips out of range behind the air compressor.

Meanwhile we are already beginning to pump some gas for those neighborhood brothers who drive to work, instead of cruising Mass Ave all night. I don't race Lionel to the pumps then, that's for sure. It's a different scene with a black behind the wheel, somehow. I'm not easy having more of them pulling in, but I'm trying to roll with it. And trying to suss, I guess, why it should seem so different? Part of it is, like I said, the way they talk. Like this morning, listening to Lionel and a coloured guy around his own age in this mint-green Coup de Ville.

"Later," says Lionel.

"Easy," says your man in the Caddy as he pulls out.

"All right," says Lionel.

It's simple English, too, but I'd be further ahead trying to learn a few words of Spanish off Rafael again.

OF COURSE FINTAN and Lionel are like brothers from the start. Eating out of each other's lunch pail, on days when Fintan bothers to bring in a lunch. Mrs Lynch, his landlady, makes up sandwiches for him sometimes, if her half-dozen cats haven't finished off the leftovers. While Lionel brings in nothing but ham on rye, day after day. Fintan never stops slagging him about that. So I tell them about these three construction workers, Paddy Englishman, Paddy Scotsman, and Paddy Irishman, who jump off this skyscraper on account of their wives always giving them the same lunch. "What I can't understand," sobs Paddy Irishman's widow at the funeral, "is Pat made his own sandwiches?"

Another day Lionel walks up to Purity Supreme at Mass Ave on his break. He comes back with a king-size bottle of Coke, and half a watermelon under his arm, walking along cool as you like. Him and Fintan proceed then to eat it, seated like a pair of eejits against the front of the garage. And if I know a couple of jokes about coloureds and watermelon, I don't tell them all the same.

Another reason they get on — besides watermelon, I mean — is that Lionel also has a good line in bullshit, wherever he gets it. For example, I mention something one afternoon about automation on car assembly lines. About how the shagging robots at least won't be leaving empty Coke bottles rattling around inside a door panel.

"You think it's coincidence?" Lionel asks. Opening his eyes that bit wider, like I've noticed he does, whenever he gets animated. "This *Terminator* flick, big fucking robot hero, comes along jus' when half of Detroit is being laid off. You think that's jus coincidence?"

Of course Fintan doesn't think that's jus' coincidence. And so the pair of them run their mouths about General Motors, then the movies, for the next hour or so. I once asked Fintan how come he knows so much about the pictures? Growing up in Donegal where I wonder had they even electricity when he was a kid?

"Killybegs," he said.

"The fishing port?" I remembered that much from my geography class.

"Nearest cinema to us. I'd thumb the seventeen miles, any chance I got."

"So fishermen like the movies?"

"Video has changed all that," Fintan said. "But when *Jaws* came out, all of Killybegs showed up every night for two weeks straight."

"Those Detroit robots will be out of a job next," Fintan starts up later, finishing off a valve job on a Ford Festiva. "Look at this so-called Ford — built in Korea with a Mazda engine? Old Henry must be turning in his grave."

"Save it till you're running for office," I tell him. The vanishing American industrial base, or something like that, being another of his hobby horses. "Long as we get paid in American dollars, it can be Martians making cars for all I care."

"Martians make Mars bars," says Fintan, who tells one then about the tape worm and the baseball bat.

Later Lionel comes in from filling up a big blue Delta 88, which reminds Fintan of an Olds he drove in Arizona. "It could pass everything on the road, except a gas station," he says. "The local sheriff had owned it previously, and his deputies used to pull me over, just to see who had bought Sheriff Brown's car."

"Jus' be black and driving any big car in Mississippi," Lionel chips in, "and every cop is gonna want to inspect your ass." That comment gets Fintan going on cops next, who he likes as much as he does priests. "Strip a roomful of cops and priests," Fintan says, "all idle and overweight, and you won't tell them apart." Real priests, that is, seeing as he has great time for Father Flanagan, who still calls by. "We need one of those Irish collection boxes for the Black Babies," I used to cod Fintan. "For Father Flanagan to empty each week." But I don't make that joke any more with Lionel on the job.

"That's a loan, Father," Fintan tells Flanagan, handing him another buck after he shows up two afternoons straight.

"You'll see that money," says Lionel, "when my hump-backed brother straightens out."

"You got that right," I tell Lionel.

"Keep giving him money," I tell Fintan, "and he'll set up here as chaplain."

The talk turns to cops again, and Lionel tells of this friend, Joe Bonet, who got stopped on the Mass Pike for speeding. "Joe starts rapping to the trooper, all Shake & Bake and say what. The guy's cross-eyed by the time he's writing Joe up. 'Bonet's the name, Officer, only the "t" is silent. Like the "l" in salmon, you follow?' Cop follows so much, he writes the ticket out to Joe Fish, and the judge throws the case outa court."

TO BE HONEST, Lionel often seems easier to figure out than Fintan, who I sometimes think has some furniture missing. "Imagine being a pond skater," he says one morning. "Surface tension, not gravity, would rule your life!"

"What's a pond skater when it's at home?" I inquire, struggling with the rusted water pump on a 1977 Pinto.

"A bug that walks on water," Fintan hands me the proper wrench. Later that afternoon I'm admiring this classy MG pulled up at the pumps. "Nice as it is," Fintan tells me, "it's no substitute for coming to know yourself."

"Piss off!" I reply, in case he's taking the mickey out of me. Meanwhile he's telling me the El Dorado is named after this Mexican gold statue. Or the Pontiac is called after some red-Indian chief. "The idea being," Fintan says, "that you too become a super-hero. Just by getting behind the wheel."

"I'm waiting for a car called Rich & Retired, so," I say. But Fintan is onto the Monte Carlos and Monacos by now.

Some days he's in foul humor, the next morning all sunshine, dispensing alms to the poor. I doubt he sleeps much, judging from the yarns about the whores and hustlers in the

Hayes Bickford on Boylston Street. Where he sometimes sits up half the night, reading some book and drinking coffee. I wonder he doesn't hang out with the rest of the low-life in the Dunkin Donuts across from us, which would save him time getting to work mornings. But then it's like he's already too far ahead of himself at times. Leaning against the garage on a slow afternoon, like he's waiting to become a mechanic again. Though other times he seems too much there. Like his carburetor's not right, and he's running on too rich a mixture.

The last week in July is so hot, the bacon fat Maggie drains into a can on top of the cooker never even congeals. Work is even more brutal, as we have to run the engines half the time we're doing a job, boosting the temperature in the bays way above 100°. Walking into the Buffet for a beer on my way home is like walking into the cool dark of a church. Around the corner, the exhaust fan from the steakhouse beside Libby's Liquors blows down the alley into the parking lot, where a couple of bums are trying to put together the price of a bottle of Thunderbird. "There's no falling out among tinkers," as my grandmother from Mayo used to say, "about who carries the budget." At work I mention how the smell of sirloins grilling must drive those poor suckers demented. It's an idle comment just, but it gets Fintan going.

"There's America, for you. The smell of steak blowing down Skid Row." The next moment he's reciting poetry again. Something about 'alleys too narrow for Chryslers', from a poem by some famous Wop poet with a name like 'Spaghetti', who Fintan met in a San Francisco bar a few years ago.

At home, the tomatoes and peppers love the heat. But there's a ban on watering your lawn, due to the lack of rain. I don't bother with the grass, but I water the vegetables and flowers late at night, trusting the neighbours either side won't call the cops. Usually the garden keeps me going weekends, but this Saturday I find myself bored pottering around. Next thing I know, I'm in the subway on my way out to Revere Beach, where I haven't gone in years. Most of the amusements are gone, but I don't bother with that side of the strip. Instead, I take a long walk along the beach, the sand black with bathers, out trying to beat the heat. I pick my way between the blankets, dodging kids, and stepping over a wino in a bright orange shirt, who's out cold in the heat. There's a kind of haze over the water from the sun, and the same heavy smell of the seaweed that's always washed up here.

On my way back, I sit down under one of the pavilions with a copy of the *Herald*, though there's nothing in it. I don't mind the noise or the crowd, but I do mind finding myself thinking about the garage on a Saturday. Or rather thinking about Fintan, who is, after all, just one of a dozen journeyman mechanics I've hired since I bought the place off Sal. I'm still not easy about Lionel, but like I said, it's Fintan who's playing on my mind. "I knew this wasn't my day," he'd announced last Tuesday, "when I couldn't see my reflection in any shop windows, walking to work."

"You're talking Disneyland," Lionel told him. But a comment like that makes me think he's as loose as a Chinaman's slipper. Then again, two hours later, he's talking nice and easy with this red-haired loon in one of the repair bays, who looked like he was about ready to blow. Wearing a green wool cap on in the ninety-five-degree heat, a fiddle tucked under his arm, and holding a brown paper bag in his other hand. We had all eyed him passing along the street the past month or so. But that morning he had walked straight into the repair bay, his engine racing and his eyes like two green laser beams. Even Lionel was keeping a VW van between himself and the guy. But Fintan had him gently by the arm, and had him moving back outside, and on his way, shortly after.

"I asked him did he know *The Bucks of Oranmore?*" Fintan said. "But right now he thinks he's John the Baptist."

"Looney tunes is all he plays," I replied.

"I hear you," said Lionel, shaking his head.

Looking out at the ocean, I wonder at Fintan having been set down on that corner of Prospect and Broadway. As if it were his task to deal with the stumble-bums along with the tune-ups. Or does he actually attract them? Birds of a feather like? Either way, there's something uncanny the way he deals with people, particularly the down-and-outs. I don't wonder any more at finding *myself* on that corner, having been there for over twenty-five years now. But Fintan is only there for a time, blown in on the breeze. Which makes me wonder all the more why I'm worrying about him.

Though maybe it's not so much worry as curiosity? As if I can't quite figure him out, unpuzzle the secret I feel everybody has? Even if you can't always see it. Or not so easily anyhow as the half-pint on the guy on the bench beside me, bulging in his trousers' pocket. Fintan drinks, smokes dope, and plays the dogs. He even quotes poetry, for Christ's sake. But I don't think any one vice has the upper hand, as it were. In other words, he's not simply an alcoholic, a pot-head, or gambler. Or a head-case, given the poems. Not that I like to pigeonhole people, it's just I can't quite draw a bead on him.

I've a thirst from the heat, so I cross the road to a hot-dog stand beside the bar where I used to work. Seated at the counter, I order a large Coke and a burger. Just to make sure that I keep thinking of work, a cop and this coloured guy a few stools down start talking cars.

"I got my Caddy," the cop tells the coloured, who looks around six-foot-six, even sitting down. "A creme puff. From a school teacher."

"What year?" the black guy asks.

"70."

"How much?"

"$3800."

"I gotta get another," goes the black guy.

"I got one for you," the cop says. "Another 70. $3200."

"I'll talk to you."

When the cop gets up, the coloured guy tells him, "You're looking lighter."

"The good life. All that JB and Scotch."

He means J & B Scotch, I think. Wondering to myself what the world's coming to, when cops are telling coloureds about their Caddys?

"How come you don't drive a Cadillac," Fintan slagged Lionel one time at work.

"My last ride's gonna be in a Caddy," Lionel laughs. "So what's my hurry?"

"A black Caddy at that," said Fintan.

"That's right," nodded Lionel. "Flesh-coloured."

Fintan then told this story about a Priest and Rabbi, always trying to outdo each other. The Priest buys a new Cadillac, so the Rabbi does too. When they meet next, the Priest tells the Rabbi, "I just baptised my car with Holy Water."

"That's nothing," says the Rabbi. "I'm just cut an inch off the tailpipe on mine!"

I order a slice of lemon meringue pie, knowing it won't be a patch on Maggie's. To my left, a couple in their early fifties begin to argue, having eaten their franks and beans in total silence.

"It was hotter yesterday," the woman says.

"You must be losing it," the guy goes. "It's six degrees higher today. Maybe more."

At least Maggie and I aren't that bad, I think, leaving the counter girl a forty-cent tip. Not that I had even inquired did she want to come out here with me. If parks have ants, beaches have sand, and picnics need neither. She was out shopping anyways, so I just left a note.

Outside the bar next door is a sign for a band, JB and Water. On my way back to the subway, I pass J & B Cleaners. That kind of coincidence often happens, but it explains nothing. It makes me think of the cop and the black guy, however, who seemed easy with each other. Which I notice, I guess, on account of hiring Lionel. Maybe it's a matter of familiarity? Like Lucy, who was in school with coloureds from kindergarten up? Even though we wanted to send her to Saint Mary's, only for the cost. Turning around, I see the Ferris wheel behind me. One of the few rides left, the roller coaster torn down years ago. Its big wheel looks smaller, the way things are meant to look when you've grown up and gone back somewhere. Or maybe it's because I'm looking at it from a distance. While that night I was hanging at the top, with the coloured lights all below, is further away still.

MONDAY I ARRIVE at the garage to find all hell has broken loose. "Mrs Kelly is waiting for you," Fintan warns me as I pass the pumps. "She finally caught on?" I ask, spying the Diamond, her husband, slumped in the passenger seat of their Dodge Aspen.

"Aye, she caught on all right," Fintan laughs.

I don't know how long we'd run that scam. All in aid of providing the Diamond with a little beer money. "Charge her for a quart of oil whenever we fill up," he kept telling me. "And I'll collect the money off yous inside?"

"She's that mean?" Fintan had asked when I explained the game to him.

"She'd give you an apple for an orchard any day."

"You son of a bitch," Mrs Kelly shouts at me in the office. "Charging me two dollars every week," her face flushed, "for an empty can of oil?" I hadn't the heart to tell her different, though it was going to cost me a steady customer. Still, life's hard enough for the Diamond without her learning the real story. JoJo Boyle claims he got his nickname because he favours diamonds when playing Twenty-Five. But you can never be sure about that kind of thing. At least he's not wearing any in his ear, like Lionel does. Barney O'Sullivan from O'Brien's was in Dingle on his holidays a few years back, where he met the Diamond's mother. "I was talking to the Diamond only last week," he said, thinking she'd be delighted to have word. "I've no son called the Diamond," the mother bit the head off Barney. "He was christened Liam." Sure, what chance had the Diamond ever, with the wife and mother two peas in a miserable pod?

After Mrs Diamond drives off, Fintan tells of an uncle in Donegal who ate only brown eggs. It proves no bother to his aunt, until the day the uncle found her boiling a white egg in a pan of tea.

"Marriage is like a military campaign," I explain.

"You and Maggie aren't so bad," says Fintan, who has come round for a meal a couple of times.

"When you're gardening, you're not fighting."

"You can't garden year round."

"So I do a few chores Saturdays. Sundays I go down the basement, where I've an easy chair, and have a couple of drinks. When the wife comes home from Mass, I give the pipes a bang with a hammer once or twice, so the whole house thinks I'm working. When I come up for the dinner, she looks at me and says, 'You've had a couple?'

"'I had a couple,' I tell her. 'Just enough to keep the rust off.'"

Lionel tells a story then about his wedding day, which sounded like an outright military campaign. His Army mates drunk, pounding on the door. Shouting 'I want to kiss the fughing bride!' Pork chops, cabbage, collard greens, and cheese pie, followed by coconut sweetbread. Gallons of Flip, this sweet wine Lionel says came in three flavours: raspberry, orange, and lime. Same colours as the Italian ices out in Revere, and probably flavoured by the same cheap syrup. He and Diane are still together, in a house on Putnam Street, west of the Port, their two sons grown. Weekends they drive out to these huge flea markets, where they walk around the tables and stalls. Looking at stuff and maybe buying one or two things. "I don't care about that," Lionel says. "But we always stop for lunch somewhere, maybe the Hilltop up on Route 1."

As marriages go, that doesn't sound too bad. I don't remember my parents doing anything together, not even

Mass. My father went to the nine o'clock, while my mother got us all out for the eleven. Even when he was in the house, it was like he wasn't really there. He took my brother and I out to Croke Park once or twice a year, but that was the height of it. Of course he probably didn't know to do it any differently. Like the starlings on Maggie's programme the other night. "Imprinted" is what she said they are. As if they have a computer chip in their head that makes them lay their eggs in another's nest. Or drive song birds away from a feeder. Imprinted is maybe what my Da was, so? He was for the birds anyway, a shedful of them in our back garden.

Though he wasn't the worst, I know that. The TV chat shows over here are full of people, giving out about their parents. But most of those griping sound like they never grew up themselves — even if some of their parents seem to have been weirdly imprinted all right! I know that isn't limited to over here, either. Whatever about the Da, it was never as bad in our house as JoJo Boyle claimed it got in Sligo. Where he used to share a bed with his father. "Mammy, I think Daddy's dead," he went into the mother one night when he was ten or so. "Oh, don't mind that, JoJo," the mother said. "Go back to bed, and we'll take him out in the morning." I don't know if I ever believed that one from JoJo, but I understood it wasn't great between his parents all the same.

After Lionel describes his wedding, Fintan says something about never working for a married couple. Which prompts Lionel to say there's worse scenarios. Such as this restaurant where he worked after first getting out of the Army. "The boss's wife was cashier, and his girl friend was waitressing, which spelt trouble for everybody. Plus we'd this crazy Hungarian cook, who hated the girl friend. He'd leave a plate on the range, then put her order on it, so she'd burn herself lifting it. One day he put a fork far enough into her behind, she needed a tetanus shot. I took a swing at him, but the boss got in between us. Scared shitless the cook was gonna spill the beans about the girl friend to his wife."

Of course, not everybody gets married in the end. Like Aunt Kate, who I stopped with in Dorchester. There was word of a fellow in her life long before I came over, but I don't know if even my mother ever learned what came of that. All I know is that every Paddy's Day she'd leave the house early, not coming back till ten at night. Even the first year or two after she left Dorchester and came to live with Maggie and me in the Port. She never let on where she went, and while it might have been the parade and church, or a sick friend, I always wondered had it something to do with that failed match? Still, she seemed happier than her sister, my mother, even if she never married. She worked for Ma Bell, looking up telephone numbers for years. Helped out with the Ladies' Sodality, and played a night of cards every Wednesday. I don't think she found it easy going back to Ireland to visit either, which she only did a few times, but we never talked of that. Boston seemed to be her home, end of story. Like she had taken root over here. She left me the house in Dorchester when she died in 1967, the day after Lucy turned three. Which was how I was able to come up with the down payment, when Sal offered to sell me the garage eight or nine years later.

FINTAN HAS HAD a girl friend, Katherine, since he started at the garage, but I understand she's always giving up on him. A nice girl from Mayo, who I first meet when she comes in for a fill-up. "She complains I'm a high-maintenance boyfriend," Fintan laughs, making out like he doesn't quite get it. That same week he asks do I want to go to a Sox game with him and Katherine on Sunday?

I've never been to Fenway, but I decide why not, and say I'll meet them at the park. I'd ask Maggie, but she's no more a ball fan than I am. The day looks lovely, not too hot, so I decide to hoof it, figuring it's about an hour's walk. There's a mess of sailboats on the Charles as I cross the Mass Ave bridge, a few wispy clouds above the Hancock Tower. I turn right on Commonwealth, not left as I usually do if I'm walking this way. In order to take in the brick residences coming up to the Boston Public Gardens, which remind me a little of the Georgian houses back home. Today however I carry on down Commonwealth the other way, into Kenmore Square, and over the railroad bridge to the park. Where I meet Fintan and Katherine at the bleachers' entrance.

We find seats about halfway up. Above what Fintan calls the bull pen, where a couple of players are throwing a ball back and forth. "Pitchers warming up," Fintan says. The park is beautiful to look at, a big expanse of bright green grass in the outfield, and a massive olive-green wall over in what Fintan says is left field. I've known for years that being "out in left field" means you haven't a clue, but this is the first time I've actually seen it. And if the player in right field seems equally out of the picture, I don't worry my head about it. As it is, I wouldn't know what any of it's called, only Fintan's explaining everything to Katherine.

After we load up with popcorn and a programme, Fintan goes down and gets beers for himself and Katherine. But drinking beer in the sun only gives me a headache, whatever about drinking it from a plastic cup, so I have an orange soda instead. I hear Katherine call it a mineral, which I haven't heard in donkeys' years. Come to think of it, a mineral was called a tonic in Boston when I first landed, only tonic has died out since. Meanwhile Katherine wants to know why it's called a bull pen, which Fintan for once can't answer.

The Red Sox are playing the Chicago White Sox. Which makes me think of the fortnight Sean Hickey and I spent trudging around the Windy City, looking for a start. We stand for the national anthem, after which Fintan tells this pitiful joke about José, Can You See? So pitiful that even Katherine refuses to laugh. I became a US citizen shortly after Maggie and I got married, but the Star Spangled Banner doesn't do much for me. Any more than the Irish anthem they used to finish up the dances with in Dublin. The game starts then, but I'm not that pushed about it. Especially as it moves at a snail's pace. I'm content just looking around at the other fans, and at the park with its huge light towers. I was mad about anything with a ball in it, growing up. But I pretty much gave up on sports when I came over. Fintan said he was so homesick at first, he bought a soccer ball just to carry around. Now, however, he's mad for the whole lot — baseball, basketball, and ice hockey even.

"Does he take you bowling?" I ask Katherine after a while.

"You must be joking!" she laughs. But nicely, so I don't end up feeling a right spare. She's about my Lucy's age. Slight, with curly brown hair, and one of those soft country accents. All of a sudden, there's this mad scramble a few rows below us for a home-run ball, which puts the White Sox three runs up. Once it settles back down, Katherine talks a bit about her job. Making pastries for this exclusive shop on Newbury Street near the Public Gardens. Sensible she is, far too sensible for Fintan.

I get the feeling he really likes her, though, on the way home. Fintan has asked me back for a beer, and though he and Katherine took the T in, we all walk back to Cambridge together. The afternoon sun has stirred up a slight breeze off the Charles, where people are jogging, cycling, walking dogs, throwing frisbees, along with just lying on blankets. Fintan and Katherine hold hands across the bridge, making plans for the beach next weekend. Passing the big MIT buildings on Mass Ave, I get this sudden pang — of envy or something like it. And suddenly I'm remembering, for the first time in years, a summer night Maggie and I went swimming in Fresh Pond, up near the Belmont line.

It was the year after we met at Revere Beach, and just before we started courting in earnest. We had no togs with us, having only come out Brattle Street from Harvard Square that far for a walk. It was Maggie who suggested we slip though a hole in the chain-link fence around the reservoir. Which we did, stripping off in the moonlight. I can still feel the small round stones underfoot. And see the soft white look of her underclothes as she waded out in the dark. Walking back along Huron Ave, we were stopped by a cop on his beat.

"You were swimming in Fresh Pond?"

"No, sir," I replied.

"So how come you're all wet?"

"We were in the grass," said Maggie without blinking.

"Luck of the Irish," the cop laughed at me, too pleased with his own wit.

It was another few months before we came close to anything like that. But I took the subway back to Dorchester that night, thinking Maggie had maybe tipped her hand?

When we hit the Square, I try to head home down Pearl Street. Fintan however insists I come back for a cold one. His room is in a four-storey brick walk-up on Norfolk Street, just behind the bowling alley where Maggie and I used to go. Only the bowling alley is some kind of African Church now, whatever they did with the lanes and pool tables. You can smell the garbage in the black plastic bags alongside Fintan's building, while inside flies circle in the cool of the hallway. The stairs could use a good sweep, and there are two or three locks on every door all the way up to the fourth floor.

It's fairly hot in Fintan's room, seeing he likes air conditioners like he does TVs. It's also absolutely spick and span, which comes as no surprise, seeing how he keeps the toilet and yard at work. And you can see he's made an effort at decorating, with bits and bobs lifted along the street on trash day. There's a picture of some sunflowers on the wall, a bookcase of paperbacks, and an Elvis Presley lamp on a small table beside the single bed in the corner.

Fintan switches on the window fan, then gets three long-neck bottles of Bud from a tiny fridge. He pulls a straight-back chair up to what looks like a fourth-hand sofa, where Katherine and I are seated. We make small talk for a while, about nothing in particular. Fintan has this habit of rubbing his fingers together, when he's making an effort at something. Which isn't often, because it's almost always spontaneous with him, though I see him doing it now. I think he's pleased at having us there, at getting the chance to play the host. But there's something almost sad in the whole scenario. For one, the room seems more like a monk's cell, than anywhere you might call home. Maybe it's the tidiness of the few pieces in it. Making it look even more sparsely furnished than it actually is? Or maybe it's that I can't help remembering a story Fintan told at work a few days before. About the puzzled look this cop gives him, after lifting him for thumbing somewhere out West.

"What's your address?" the cop asked.

"No fixed abode, officer."

"No what?" said the cop, who wasted no time arresting him for vagrancy.

Looking around at the sunflowers and Elvis lamp, it strikes me his digs has "no fixed abode" written all over it. Funny enough, a minute later Fintan is telling Katherine about the Octoberfest in Munich, where he lived for a time. About how the hotels there simply give their guests a tag with their address, so a taxi can bring them home, no matter how stocious.

What started out a nice day at the ballpark has me melancholy enough on my way home. It looks like a thunderstorm is brewing; the air is that bit heavier, and the breeze cooler now, more restless. I get home just before it starts to belt down, hard gusts of rain that'll only do the garden good. There's a note on the kitchen table from Maggie, who has gone over to her sister Patti. I make myself a chicken sandwich for my supper, giving a few bits to Guzzles, who is determined to trip me up. The rain stops as quickly as it began, leaving a bit of a breeze which shifts the steam from a pot of pickles Maggie has left simmering, its shadow shimmering like smoke against the refrigerator door. Everything seems both sun-splashed and rain-splashed: the giant begonias on the window ledge are glistening, and there's a smear of rainbow on the kitchen wall from a tiny prism Maggie has hanging in the window. The whole room bathed in this late-afternoon golden light, which only makes me all the more glum.

As Luis and Fatima downstairs have gone to the Cape for the weekend, I take my sandwich down to the front porch. Where I sit and watch the rain dripping off the trees. It's too wet to go out back, but I also know this is one of those rare times when the garden won't do me any good. And, while I know it makes no sense, I don't like going out there when I'm feeling like this. Like it won't do the plants any good to have me moping about.

Sitting on, I think of Katherine looking around Fintan's room. Taking in the hot plate and bath towel on the back of the door, and probably seeing fuck-all prospects in it. Yet she's sweet on him all right. And there's something about Fintan that makes women want to do for him. I noticed Maggie took to him quick when he first came over for a Sunday dinner. Mrs Lynch, his landlady, is the same. Fixing him bag lunches and so on. A thin, chain-smoking widow, she eyeballed Katherine and me going up the stairs this afternoon. Trying to suss if we were Fintan's long-lost family or something. What I think they all miss, however, is that Fintan is at heart a man's man — as most of us are.

Which probably explains why Maggie's out, and I'm sitting here solo on the front porch of a Sunday evening? Or why she watches TV most evenings, while I've my nose in a magazine. Or a book even, though nothing heavy like what Fintan reads. Even if it started different, back at the top of the Ferris wheel, it's rolled round to this. *Rotha Mór an tSaoil: The Big Wheel of Life*, which Fintan said they had to read at school. About this Donegal fellow who travelled around America and Canada.

The Irish we did in school was all about culchies, too. None of who ever travelled more than seven miles from a cow's tail in their life, or so far as I could decipher from the Irish. There was a crossing guard on Lucy's way to school, an old codger from Clare, the odd morning I used to walk her when she was little. Mr Clancy, from Ennistymon, who'd greet me with a *Dia dhuit* any morning he saw me. The fact I had as much Irish as I have Spanish must've been a disappointment to him. Though I at least taught Lucy the *Dia is Muire dhuit* with which to answer him.

It must have some inner tube, the Wheel of Life, all the same? Or does it puncture itself, for a JoJo Boyle, say? Or blow out sometimes, like the Irish bartender who got shot in New York last week? I can imagine the red face on that bastard Lyons, trying to beat the Irish into us, had we asked him something like that. "What if there's no tread left on the Wheel of Life, sir?" Myself, I figure I'm good for another 30,000 miles, that much tread left anyhow. Nor am I — despite hanging out today with Fintan and Katherine — wishing I was thirty years younger, with it all still to play for. Having had a child, like Lucy, teaches you the foolishness of that. Nor can it be always skinny-dipping in Fresh Pond, either. Though maybe it's the easy laughs to those early times you miss?

I wonder — though I don't like admitting it — whether the trip out yesterday to Tippy's Garden Center on Route 2 isn't what's working on me? It was nothing special, just one of a number of runs I might make on the weekend. Only I had asked Maggie did she want to come along. She's low, like I said, ever since Lucy left for California, but yesterday she's even quieter than usual.

"The plaster squirrels are only $2.95," I told her, figuring it's her kind of wildlife. She knows I was teasing, but she said nothing. I got my bag of mulch, then spied these tiger lilies on our way out.

"You want one of them?" figuring it's the kind of indoor plant she'd like.

"It'll be dead before we get it home in this heat," she said, so I left it. Any more offers will only lead to our having words. Though I suppose I should have been happy she didn't want one of those Virgins on a Half-Shell for a corner of the garden? Or "grottoes" as I heard old Tippy call them, the blue paint of Our Lady's robe already peeling off the plaster. I guess foolish is what I'm now feeling — for thinking a trip out to Tippy's was any kind of an outing to begin with. So I just sit on, watching the last of the sun on the rain-soaked maples, and wondering how twenty-two years of marriage wouldn't wear any couple down?

THE NEXT WEEK at work we have the radio tuned to the ball game any afternoon the Sox are playing. Now in second place just two games behind the Orioles. I don't follow the play-by-play, though now I can at least picture a double off the wall in left, or a pop-up to the pitcher. Still, I prefer the baseball to the tapes that have been blaring for the last month. Either Lionel's jungle music, or Fintan's diddly-eye, diddly-eye. Neither of which are a patch on the Verdi Sal used to play. I understand fiddle music is all the rage now in Ireland. Even Dublin, where we rarely heard it growing up.

There were even lads playing the fiddle in The Plough & The Stars further up Mass Ave, towards Putnam Square, the night I met Fintan there for a drink. I'd heard about the place for a few years, but never bothered my arse to check it out. It's a different bar to O'Brien's all right. Brightly lit, and no TV in sight. It's not one of those yuppie places either, with a lot of brass and potted ferns. Just stools, long benches, some tables, and Guinness on draft. But it's no more my cup of tea, all the same. Too effing loud, for starters. Plus the crowd is far younger than myself. Students a lot of them, and few, if any, Irish accents that I can make out over the din.

Anyhow, we now have just the radio going at work, no more tapes. After I told the lads I was running a garage, not a music hall. The radio is tuned to the talk-show nuts when the Sox are idle. Or the pop stuff which I don't even hear. The weather, meanwhile, is still up there in the nineties, making for a haze over the sun as soon as it rises. The caramel from the NECCO factory smells like summer itself as I reach the Square mornings, sweet and heavy on the air. Even the sunflowers in this yard on Magazine Saint look like they've had enough sun. While the patch of weeds in our lot next to the alley is totally burnt-out, except for a handful of blue chicory. By ten o'clock it's so hot you can see the fumes from the hose-nozzle, shimmering like a mirage as you're pumping gas.

We get a laugh on Tuesday, when a young one goes by in a yellow tee-shirt. IT'S NOT THE HEAT... it says on the front, with IT'S THE HUMIDITY!! on the back. That same afternoon, this blonde pulls up in a red Triumph for a fill-up. She hops out to get a Coke, showing off her purple satin athletic shorts and a tight white tee-shirt with "Recreation Department" lettered across the chest. "You can say that again," laughs Fintan, as she hops back into her car. Fintan, who rarely comments on any of the women passing by, unlike Evangelis, who, despite his limited English, had a mouth like a sewer.

We all made our remarks in Ireland, one to another, but I remember my discomfort my first year here, at the crudeness of the lads on the construction site, whenever a woman walked by. Of course it's a different world now, the TV and movies full of what you used to only see in some magazines, never mind the language.

Mario Andretti comes by next to freshen up. Hauling himself in and out of his wheelchair, parked outside the toilet door. Fintan says the word on the street is that Mario can walk. But I wonder, seeing he has the built-up biceps and shoulders of somebody truly chair-bound. Lionel goes over then and chats with him a bit. About Vietnam I reckon?

"Man, what you doing?" I hear Lionel shouting at Fintan an hour later. Who is after pouring an ice-cold Coke down the toilet.

"We're out of Ajax."

"So you drink Ajax, when you can get it?" Lionel shakes his head in disgust.

I send Fintan down to Purity Supreme for a can of Ajax. When he comes back, we swap stories about making do. Condensed milk for a leaking radiator, or sawdust into a banjaxed transmission or rear axle. Of course rear axles themselves are disappearing off the newer models. Which is probably just as well, seeing sawdust isn't so easy to come by anymore? Fintan tells then about thumbing a lift in Illinois, with a fellow who had just put a couple of raw eggs into his radiator. The smell of them cooking made Fintan so queasy, he asked the guy to let him out.

We move on to home cures next. Like the white-bread poultice my mother used to wrap around our fingers for a splinter, say. Fintan who, like I said, never talks much about

Donegal, knows loads of herbal cures his grandmother swore by. Dock berries for a cough, and wild garlic in whiskey and honey for a cold. Which sounds like a waste of good whiskey, though I suppose Sal would have thought it a waste of good garlic? It's all wasted on Fintan anyway, who told me he only used drugs for recreation, after I offered him an aspirin once for a headache. Still, I'm thinking of putting in a small herb garden at home, ever since Maggie started trying out stuff she's seen on the cookery programmes. "Fresh herbs are better," she keeps telling me, pronouncing it "erbs".

"I'll grow some herbs, so," I tell her, keeping the "h" in it like we do in Ireland. I've gotten better over the years, about seasonings and spices. Though I still can't abide caraway seeds, which my mother used to put in everything, since she couldn't get anything else during the war. I even put in some coriander this spring, only the cat has it flattened from lying on it. Stoned, no doubt, from whatever dope is in it.

Meantime Lionel is after me to keep the toilet door locked, Ajax or not.

"I found a syringe behind the hopper last week."

"You better lean on Brother Fintan," I tell him. Who is still unlocking the door for his Apostles.

"All those bums gonna give you white guys a bad name."

It's only after Lionel says that, that I realise the riffraff coming by are, in fact, all white. While I would have no doubt noticed their colour, if we had coloured winos hanging round. One coloured who did come by last week, his too-big shoes curling up at the toes, got a real bum's rush from Lionel. Who wouldn't let him use the jacks even.

"I don't need no junkie slobbering on me."

"No sympathy?" I needle him, surprising myself.

"He knows where he can find sympathy," Lionel snorts.

"In the dictionary?"

"You got that right. Between shit and Shinola."

The heat is making people raggedy all right. Or at least so I'm thinking. And, sure enough, Lionel has a few words with this white Cougar at the pumps, just before we close. I recognise the guy, who comes in for gas occasionally. A short, baldy type. With a cigar stub, like a dog turd, always in the corner of his mouth. Though maybe I only think it looks that way now, after he's started something with Lionel?

I can't get out of Lionel what happened. But Fintan, wheeling in a rack of tires, says the guy passed some racial comment.

"You OK?" I ask.

"Fuck him," Lionel says.

"And the horse he rode in on."

"'S'all right," Lionel says, and I let it go at that.

I'M IN GOOD FORM the next morning, having counted twenty-three morning glories on the trellis out back. I've never had much luck with them before this year, whatever I was doing wrong. Staring at them, I see the blossoms are exactly as advertised: a glory of the morning, their fluted blue trumpets tinged with violet. When I come back in the kitchen, Maggie tells me they begin to wilt by early afternoon. And the fact that she comments on them cheers me, too.

"Are they Heavenly Blues?" Fintan asks at work, which knocks me for a loop.

"What do you know about flowers?"

"I know my morning glories," Fintan laughs. "Problem is the seeds are coated with strychnine. So you puke like a dog, if you don't soak them first."

"Say what?" says Lionel, looking as puzzled as myself.

"The Aztecs used them too," Fintan says. "The head priest ate them. Then peed into a gourd, out of which the rest of them drank to get off."

"I'll stick to reefer," Lionel says.

"Whatever you're having yourself," Fintan shrugs.

I might have known it was a drug thing, hardly gardening. But the idea of eating morning glory seeds is so bizarre, I ask Fintan about it later.

"I only did them once, with a mate in California. We ate a couple of tablespoons each. Sitting on the beach staring at the sunset. The best part was feeling the sound of the waves breaking. Rippling up and down your skin."

"Fuck that," I say.

"Synaesthesia," laughs Fintan, giving me another of his twenty-five cents words. "Your senses get screwed up, and you start tasting colours, or seeing noises."

I mostly don't want to know about pot and pills. Never mind the hard stuff like smack. It's a matter of age, I suppose. Drugs being, for our crowd, the cough bottles Joe Maguire drank in the toilet at O'Brien's. In between the Stingers he drank at the bar, before that night he swept the glasses into the ice trough, and they had to pull O'Brien off him. It's also a matter of the poison you're used to. Which in my case has always been hootch. And hootch is hard enough to keep in line, without trying out powders and weeds. I'd a kid helping out a few years back, a real hophead. Stinking of pot, which you can't miss, each time he toked up in the back room. We did the odd bit of body work then, panel beating if you like. And that kid would sit hammering the same spot for hours on end.

Neither Fintan nor Lionel are using anything on the job, however, which is the way I like it. Though Fintan's always offering me a piece of what he calls "buzz gum". Made out of some seed from the Amazon.

"Better for you than caffeine."

"Anything beats *that* caffeine," says Lionel, pointing at our coffee pot.

"I don't chew seeds," I tell Fintan. "Just plant them."

"Try one, Mickey. Over the counter stuff. FDA approved."

"FU, if you don't mind," I tell him. "And go pump some gas while you're at it."

The incident with one of the looney-tunes happens that afternoon. After Lionel found the syringe, I had told Fintan the toilet door stays locked, end of story. Anyhow, around three o'clock, I look up from under the hood of a Hornet. To see the same nasty-looking streak of misery who'd had words with Evangelis in June, shouting something about the toilet at Lionel in the office.

It spells trouble, so I grab a long-tailed wrench and head over. And sure enough I hear "Nigger" twice, before I even get there. And before I see the hunting knife the guy is holding on Lionel, with about five feet between them.

Next thing I know, Lionel lifts this empty bottle off the counter with his left hand. Keeping his eyes on the knife, he steps back and gives the bottle a fierce rap on the counter. And

I'm fucked if the bottom doesn't break off, giving him all kinds of jagged edges to work with.

"Things go better with a big, big Coke," he tells the guy, holding the bottle by its neck, and leaning forward onto the balls of his feet. Which is as good as you get at the movies, I think. I look across the street, but there's never a cop having donuts when you need one. The fight, however, has pretty much gone out of the scabby dipstick. And when Fintan comes up behind him at the outside door, holding a tire iron, he slips the knife into his hip pocket.

I tell him I'll call the cops, if I ever see his ass again. I then tell Lionel to take the afternoon off.

"No way."

"I'm paying you to take it off."

"Pay the deposit on the bottle," he tosses it in the bin, "you wanna pay something."

"Go home, will you?"

"I go home every time some PWT calls me 'nigger', I may as well stay in bed."

I don't know what to say to that. Apart from wondering what a PWT is, whenever it's at home?

I do know Mrs Fitzgerald is collecting her Hornet at half-five, but I sit on for another minute with Lionel. Who suddenly starts telling me about his father, who lives with him and Diane in a granny flat converted out of their side-porch.

"'Pappy, we's black now,' I told him once. 'No longer coloured.' 'Well, I'm still coloured,' he says. Like that's that. A week later I take him to get a credit card in Lechmere's, where the salesgirl checks this box for "black" under race."

"'Black?' he says, 'Black?' And before I can stop him, he's a shoe off and up on the counter. 'That's black!' he says. 'Do I look that colour?'"

"'Put your shoe on, Pappy,' I tell him. 'Put that black shoe back on your coloured foot.'"

I think about telling Lionel how tinkers back home became itinerants and then travellers. For those anyhow who don't call them knackers. Or so Fintan says. But there's no way I can manage that. Like there's simply too much ocean between us. Even if he's seated just across from me, talking about his Pappy.

It happens we have a house full of tinkers just down Prospect Street from the garage. From Romany, only they're called gypsies over here. There must be fifteen of them, living in the one place. The men all drive late-model pickups. Going door to door, looking to pave your driveway, same as in Ireland. "Four inches of the best tar-macadam, Boss!" Only you'd want to be out there with a ruler while they're pouring. The women call by the garage, selling paper flowers which Fintan sometimes buys, depending on his humour. Bare legs in slippers, and mismatched blouses and skirts. All reds and yellows, clashing so loud you can hear them coming.

One of the men came in for a tune-up last year. Once we had it done, he took the truck around the block to see how it runs. That's the last we saw of him, of course. Until last week when he showed up, looking for the same again.

"Not till you pay for last year's," I told him.

"Oh, fuck!" he goes. Or something like it in Romanian. Having figured, I suppose, that we'd never remember him? But he settled his arrears, and paid again when we finished tuning up his truck. I remember Uncle Derek having great time for them in Dublin. Haggling for hours over the price of some motor he was selling out of his back lane. My father, however, would hunt them from the door. "They're the boys'll clean you out," he'd say. "Hens and all." Even if we'd fuck-all hens, only canaries, in Marino. The brother Jack is one of those who calls them knackers now — which is Irish for "nigger" I guess.

I go back under the Hornet's hood that afternoon, but I can't help thinking about Lionel. Nor is it his fancy work with the Coke bottle that's playing on me. You could only admire that, seeing as how the other guy pulled a knife first. Besides, there wasn't even a trace of temper off him. Unlike somebody like Sean Hickey who came over with me, say. And who had a hair trigger if you crossed him. Take the job we were once on in Brookline, renovating this big house? There was some problem with the electric bill, but it was between the builder and Boston Edison. Nothing to do with us hired hands. Still, when the linesman pulled up in his yellow truck to cut off the power, Sean stuck this pneumatic nail-gun out the second-storey window, and squeezed off a round at the poor bastard halfway up the pole. The Brookline PD was there fifteen minutes later, but the ganger had by then already fired Sean's arse. Which was parked on a bar stool, waiting for me, down in Brookline Village.

What's puzzling me this afternoon is something else entirely about Lionel. It's like I can't square his earrings, tatoo and shaved head with his taking the wife to weekend flea markets. Or getting his Da a credit card? It's not that I think Lionel's lace curtain, but he hardly living a pirate's life either. Even if he looks like a bloody buccaneer. If I bother to think about it, there are a handful of black families living quiet lives around us down in the Port. But then again I'm not sure I want to think about it. Because those domesticated coloureds won't boost your chances with any hopped-up black young buck you meet on the street at night. Anyhow, I'm closing up before I think to ask Fintan what PWT means, but for once he hasn't a clue.

So I don't think any more about it. Instead I head home to pick some early runner beans. Which Maggie is going to cook in olive oil and garlic, with sliced almonds. Like she saw on this Italian cookery show. Sal used to bring in things like that for lunch, which I wouldn't even look at. I find Maggie out in the garden, however. All excited over what looks like a dirty grey sock, hanging in the willow tree by the back fence.

"It's a Baltimore oriole's nest."

"They're playing the Sox tonight."

But Maggie pays that no mind. "They've a lovely orange patch on their wings."

"It must be over at Fenway," I say, after we wait a few minutes in vain. "With the rest of the team." Yet the fact that the bird's in our garden — and not on the TV — cheers me up, even if I haven't seen it yet. What's more, the beans at supper are tasty enough, once you get used to the oil.

It's my turn now to surprise the Morning Glory expert. Who is doing the crossword the next morning when I get to work. And funny enough, it has to do with birds, though not orioles.

"A four-letter word for the offspring of two different birds or plants?"

"Mule," I tell him.

"I said bird, not beast."

"It's what you call a hybrid bird. If you mate a canary with a goldfinch, say."

"Mule?"

"M-U-L-E," I enjoy spelling it out for him.

"My Da kept them," I explain. "Canaries, linnets, zebra finches."

Fintan is a terror for anything new, so he pumps me now about breeding birds. I haven't thought about that shed with its bird cages in ages. But it's all there, tucked away in the back of the head.

"He used to spread birdlime for any cats," I tell Fintan. "Then go after them with a hatchet. My Mam made him stop that, but he kept a sling handy, along with a supply of rusty nuts he got from some scrap-yard. Four sharp edges on each of those little suckers. He was handy with the sling too. So much so that any two-eyed cat you saw on the road was likely a tourist."

"A right St Francis," Fintan says.

"We buried him on a bitter day in February," I finish up. "But I swear to God there was one bush near the grave, absolutely filled with birds."

"I hear you," Lionel says, who I can tell likes that bit.

We have no cars in the bays this morning, so I go on and tell about the bird-market held off Patrick Street every Sunday morning. Just a walk down from the Jacob's Biscuits factory on Bishop Street. And the story my father told of the man who bought a canary there. Only he discovers it has a leg missing when he gets home. He goes back the following Sunday, but the seller's having none of it. "That canary had two legs when you bought it," he tells your man, "so you can fuck off about getting your money back!" "That sparrow was a canary when you bought it!" was probably what they said, too, after the dye they had used wore off the feathers.

I don't know when the last time was I'd thought of those birds behind our house. Or the bird mart, for that matter, where my father took Jack and me a few times. We didn't give a shite about the birds, but it was lovely going into town early on the bus, with hardly any cars about. And the chance of an ice-cream wafer, if the Da was happy with a bird he'd found. Come to think of it, he probably cared for those birds something in the way I like to garden? Seated for hours at a time, watching their antics in the big communal cage along one wall of the shed, with a smaller cage for any hens sitting on eggs. All those chaffinches and linnets keeping company with his starling-self, I suppose?

Later that evening I'm out in the garden, weeding. Luis from downstairs comes out for a chat, and I give him a mess of onions from the garden for Fatima. He's headed in, when I think to ask is the kitchen faucet I fixed leaking again? He turns to say it isn't, and as he stands there in the dying light, a clump of onions in either hand, I'm suddenly seeing that snapshot of him with the two Angolans again.

I stay at the weeding until it's finally too dark to see what I'm pulling. Still reluctant to go in, I wander over for a last look at the nicotiana I put in from last year's seeds. This summer it's like a plant from another planet. So large it's like having somebody else in the garden with you at night, when it opens up for moths. Spreading out like some kind of ghostly bush, the scent from its white flowers heavy on the night air. Maggie had a programme on recently, all about moths. How they prefer to fly about at night, unlike butterflies. Resting with their wings horizontal, and so forth. And sure enough, this night I spot two flying about the nicotiana.

Maybe it's the nocturnal moths, or the talk earlier about my Da's birds. Either way, I'm suddenly remembering this picture that hung last year in the Salvation Army shop on Mass Ave, just down from the Post Office. *Nighthawks* it was called, though I don't remember the painter's name. The picture had me hooked, though, and I used to stare at it in the window any time I was passing, till I had it nearly memorised.

The more I looked, too, the odder it seemed, though it was really pretty simple. Just a late-night café, with a couple facing you at the counter, talking to a guy in a white jacket and cap behind it, and another fellow at the counter with his back to you. The guy with the woman looks like a hard-boiled Bogart or John Garfield type. Fedora hat and holding a cigarette — a reporter or a plainclothes cop maybe — though I didn't see any donuts, only coffee. Meanwhile the woman, a redhead in a red dress, is examining her nails. She seems kind of bored, though her other hand is practically touching the guy's, so maybe they're doing all right? The soda jerk also looks happy enough.

At first I thought it was maybe the fellow sitting alone, hunched forward in another fedora, which made the picture seem so lonely. Half of himself lost in the blackness you see beyond the big plate-glass window. However, the more I studied it up, the more I saw how unreal the whole scene was. For openers, there's this lime-green colour all over the sidewalk outside the café, which even a sodium-vapour streetlamp doesn't give you at night. Furthermore, the light on the brick shopfront across the street looks like sunshine — even though it's supposed to be late at night?

Once you see that, you also notice the footpaths and street are absolutely spotless. And there's nothing in the shops beyond the café, aside from a cash register. All of which, once you see it, is entirely unreal. It's almost like the painting's a codology, except for the feeling in it? And the fact it's a painting, I suppose, and not a photograph. There's nothing in the flats above those shops, either. No curtains, blinds, or people: only a slice of that same strange green light in one window. And hardly anything in the café itself, beyond the people. Just these two huge coffee urns, a few salt & pepper shakers, and three of those thick white coffee mugs like Maggie and I used to have. Which we got in fact from that very Salvation Army shop, just after we got married. Getting elbowed by old ladies rooting through boxes of chipped cereal bowls and plastic glasses.

Of course we have matched sets of everything at home now, twenty-odd years on. Still, Lucy wrote how she had outfitted her Sacramento kitchen from a Salvation Army shop. Which made me proud of her, somehow. As if being born in the Land of Milk & Plenty hasn't entirely turned her head. "Give us this day our Daily Bread," was how Uncle Derek said you prayed in America. "Plus three eggs!"

Somehow the eggs bring Fintan next to mind, as I stand there this night, watching the moths circle the nicotiana. No better nighthawk than Fintan, hanging out till all hours in that Hayes Bickford across the river. Were you to paint his all-nighter, however, you wouldn't have whites only in it. As it was, I nearly bought that picture last year. Though I can imagine the look on Maggie, had I come home with a painting under my arm. Never mind one with a redhead in a red dress. Which is another thing, she'd point out, that you'd never see in real life.

Coiling the hose, I think of Jackie Callaghan from Roscommon, playing music low into the wee hours, when he lived below us. Or the coloured guys who cruise Mass Ave all night in their cars. Even the cripple who lives in his 1970 Plymouth, or Mario Andretti in his wheelchair behind Libby's Liquors. Or the other low-rent lads, drifting from Nighthawk Alley beside the garage into the 24-hour Dunkin Donuts across the street. All of them nighthawks, trying to steady the nerve with cigarettes or coffee, or deaden it with alcohol. All with an edge to themselves, either uprooted or rootless, transplants that somehow didn't take. Noting a couple of marrows that need eating, I decide to call it a night, leaving the garden to the nicotiana and the moths.

IT BEGINS THEN in August to go seriously wrong for Fintan. I can pinpoint the morning he starts to slip, even.

"What's new?" I greet him.

"Same shit, different day," he replies, which is not his usual style.

He's also muttering again about not seeing his reflection anywhere. "Fuck me, it's Dracula!" Lionel laughs, making a cross with his fingers. That foolishness only unsettles me again, however. And while Fintan has always kept a bottle in the back room, for any Apostle in a bad way, he's beginning now to hit it himself.

"You're going to end up in O'Brien's," I warn him after a week of this carry-on. "Watching *Candlepins for Cash*."

"Just enough to keep the rust off," he replies. Later that day, two kids come by looking for used spark plugs. To make hash pipes, would you believe? "Fuck off," Fintan tells them, which — while not bad advice — is once more not his usual style. I notice the toilet isn't so clean anymore, either.

I'm wondering now if maybe the drink has the upper hand, after all? Even though that's usually a symptom of something else gone wrong. Like white exhaust, indicating your antifreeze is getting into your oil. I don't mean like a medical symptom in any case. Because I don't hold with alcoholism being a disease. It fucks up your health all right, like a disease. But I don't think it starts as a sickness per se. Call it what you like, you need to either manage the fucking stuff, else leave it alone. I still laugh at Barney O'Sullivan, one of the regulars down at O'Brien's, going into the basement of St Mary's years ago. The AA lads were sitting in a circle, doing their Twelve-Step business, when Barney came down the stairs.

"Good man, Barney!" they shouted. "Delighted you've seen the light!"

"Well, you guys can just fuck off," said Barney, "cuz I'm here to sign up for softball!"

Fintan's drinking slows down after a week or so. But even days when he's cheery now, there's an edge to it — as if his engine were racing or something. Yesterday we're both under the bonnet of this Ford Fairlane, when I ask him for a wrench. For fuck's sake," he snaps, "it's testicles I have, not tentacles!" And only for I laughed first, I'd have sorted him out then and there.

"They're going to bury you in that Buick," he later tells this customer so fat he can hardly walk. While Lionel and I both hold our breath, till the guy decides to laugh. Something's clearly out of whack, but people, unlike cars, don't have timing belts you can adjust. Or little red lights like a washing machine, indicating an overload.

He calls in sick one Tuesday, the first time that's happened since he started. I can't grumble about that, but I don't like the two characters that come round, looking for him. The first is a little guy, around Fintan's age, with a wee Northern accent. Belfast probably, though I've lost my ear for that kind of thing by now. He's short, like I said, but wiry. Not much flesh on him, but what's there is all muscle. His hair is short, back and sides, and he's wearing these faded but clean jeans, and a black tee-shirt. He just asks for Fintan, then leaves. There's nothing really out of order in it, but the encounter gets up my nose all the same. Making me wonder, suddenly, is Fintan a Provo along with being a Commie and an Anarchist?

I'm not even sure the second guy that afternoon is looking for Fintan. But there's something odd about him too. Around forty, with a baldy head and these big swollen hands you sometimes see on fishermen. Though if he fishes for a living, I'm the next Polish Pope. And this guy is Irish, too, though you only hear it in a few words. Not that he says much either. Just drives in and buys five gallons worth of High Test. After paying for the gas, he asks can we rotate his tires? Which, if you're looking for somebody, buys you another twenty minutes to hang around for just ten bucks. Though maybe I'm only imagining he has something to do with Fintan? Giving him a cloak and dagger, just because he doesn't let on he's Irish too?

I mention the hard man from the North the next day, but Fintan says he's just somebody he met in The Black Rose down by Haymarket Square. Neither guy comes around again, either. So by the end of the week, I'm wondering is it women trouble that's maybe making him squirrely? As I already know that Katherine threw in the towel not long after that Sunday at Fenway Park.

"She said I was like a K-Mart Blue Light Special," Fintan told me the day after she dumped him.

"Huh?" I said. Not following him, as happens half the time.

"You know, like an impulse purchase?" he grinned. "That marked-down toolbox you don't really need, and you regret buying before you have it home?"

It sounds more like his usual bullshit than something Katherine would say. But I sense he's hurt all the same. He's seeing another Irish girl then, for a week or so. Joey, a ditsy blonde from Phibsboro. A right space cadet, who calls by for him at closing time a couple of afternoons. I doubt it's serious either way, and a week later I hear Fintan telling Lionel that Joey's taken up with this professional soccer player from Mozambique. Who plays for a Toronto team, and in Monterrey, Mexico, in winter.

"Cat makes some serious money?" asks Lionel.

"He'd his first million made at sixteen," Fintan says.

"So what's Joey see in him?" Lionel laughs.

"Fucked if I know," Fintan grins. "One-hundred-dollar dinners? Plane tickets to Acapulco?"

"Any Coke?" Lionel asks.

"Bags of it," Fintan replies. Which is when I twig it's the white powdery stuff they're on about. And not Ajax, either.

I figure Fintan's not that bothered this time. But I tuck into him the next morning anyhow. Remind him he's getting decent wages, some of which he might be saving.

"Why so, Mickey?" he asks. "Long as I'm making enough to pay my bar bill and the rent?"

"Just so you're happy," I want to say, "with that Blue Light overhead." But I don't. It's none of my business, and I'm not looking to adopt a son either. "I couldn't get fucked with a fistful of fifties," I hear him tell Lionel that afternoon. Which is particularly crude for Fintan. As much the booze, as him, talking.

Two days later, pumping gas, I hear this bellowing in the garage bays. Inside I find Mario Andretti seven feet up on the lift. Cursing a blue streak, while Fintan pokes a grease gun underneath his wheelchair.

"Get him the Christ down," I yell. "Before he falls and breaks his goddamn neck."

"Not to worry, Mickey," Fintan says, "I locked his wheels before I took him up."

"You're pushing it!" I warn Fintan. Who hits the air handle which lowers Mario, wheelchair and all. Mario's all shook up, whatever about the bottle in his lap, his tongue moving back and forth like a windshield wiper.

"No drinking and driving," Fintan admonishes as Mario wheels off down the alley next to us. But it doesn't strike anybody as funny. Watering my tomatoes that night, however, I decide a stunt like that at least differs from indifference. Which is more like what most of us feel for the Marios out there?

Sunday is lovely. Bright sun, but a good fifteen degrees cooler. I watch Guzzles out the kitchen window, chasing another tom over a neighbour's garage, before deciding to go for a walk. I end up crossing the Charles again, turning east towards the Boston Gardens. To check out the flower beds, which I haven't seen since they were all tulips and narcissus in the spring. The swan boats are chock-a-block with families, and I'm buying a choc-ice from a kid with a pushcart, when I spot this bum asleep on the grass just off the footpath.

Maybe it's the purple Doc Martens I recognise first. Anyhow, looking again, I see it's Fintan all right. Walking over to him, I see his Walkman lying there, where anyone could grab it. I push it closer to him with my foot, then walk away. Too embarrassed at having found him lying there. Nor do I mention it when he shows up for work on Monday, still looking like he hasn't seen a bed.

He pulls himself somewhat together, however, over the next week or so. The Docs polished once more. And nicely ironed tee-shirts even, underneath his coveralls, making me wonder might Joey be back from Mexico? The on-the-job drinking has stopped also, judging by the level of the bottle in the back room. Tequila, which I wouldn't touch in a fit, though Fintan swears by it.

"Cactus juice," says Lionel. "Sunrise in Margaritaville."

"From the agave cactus," Fintan nods. "Pulque and mescal are distilled from the same plant." As if to show his time in Arizona had been well-spent. Except pulque, as Fintan describes it, sounds more fermented than distilled, a greenish sour kind of slop. Which must be the Mexican equivalent of Boone's Farm or Old Duke. Or Old Puke, both favourites of the lads in the carpark behind Libby's. The best tequila, says Fintan, has a worm at the bottom of the bottle, just to boost sales, no doubt. "Tequila's more a drug than a drink," he adds. Which figures from a guy who eats seeds to get a buzz on.

FALL

SEPTEMBER comes, and the heavy heat lifts at last. I'm delighted to see the back of it, but Fintan is already pissing and moaning about the winter.

"New England winters aren't the sunny Southwest either," I say. Just to cheer him up.

"Jaysus, I nearly froze to death in Arizona two years ago," he says. "I was thumbing in the mountains above Flagstaff, when it began to snow serious. It got dark, so I started walking just to keep warm. An hour later I finally spot this Esso station up ahead. I was so cold I could have drunk antifreeze and survived, but once the kid there realised I hadn't walked in to rob him, he let me sleep in the ladies' room. Which is spotless, thank God. I stuffed some newspaper in the crack under the door, and wrapped up in the rest of it. The manager showed up early the next morning, and I ended up working twelve-hour shifts there for the next month. Eating at a little truck-stop diner a mile down the road, and sleeping on a cot in back, until I thawed out enough to head off again."

"I thought Arizona was desert and rattlesnakes?" says Lionel. Giving a little shiver as he says snakes.

"Nothing for miles around that gas station but pine forest," Fintan replies.

The next Saturday I take Maggie down to the Stop & Shop on Memorial Drive to do the week's grocery shopping. Saturdays have been slow, so I had let Fintan and Lionel toss to see who works today, while I take it off. It's muggy again, but overcast, with a mist hanging like smoke in the trees along

97

the river. The store is air-conditioned, too cold in fact. And too frigging big, also. I remember being amazed at the supermarkets when I first came over. Tons of fruit and produce, while getting a banana growing up in Dublin had been a treat. I found it too much choice altogether, and I couldn't get out of the shops fast enough. Of course there's not much difference now between here and the big Irish supermarkets. Or so says Maggie, who's been back more recently than me.

Anyway, I'm hurrying her along, when this cantaloupe suddenly comes rolling past me and under a bin of broccoli. I look up, and there's Lionel. Looking part of the Fruit & Produce in this blue flowery Hawaiian shirt. Plus white jeans, blue boat shoes, and a Panama hat with a red band on his baldy head.

"Yo, Mickey!" he retrieves the melon. "Just practicing my bowling."

"You'll be on *Cantaloupes for Cash* yet," I go to shake hands with him. Only he slaps my palm, like I was a ball player or something. Which leaves me wondering can I ever get away from work? Like I'll see Fintan next, sleeping it off in the lettuce bin. Lionel's Diane pushes up their basket next, while Maggie comes back to see what's holding me up. So now it's introductions all around, which begins awkward, but gets easy. Bitching about the prices, and peering into each other's baskets. Diane looks lively, a few years younger than Lionel. Wearing this red and green sun-suit that shows she's a handsome woman yet.

"I want to thank you Mickey," she tells me. "For keeping this boy out of my hair." After which they mosey off toward the meat counter. Looking for a side of sandwich ham, no doubt, for Lionel's lunches.

"Lionel seems nice," Maggie says as we wheel down the pet-food aisle.

"Lionel's all right," I agree, wondering if Fintan even bothered to turn up at the garage this morning, seeing that he lost the toss.

Maggie will be starting work herself on Monday. Part-time sales clerk in Corcoran's on Mass Ave, which is what I figure she needs. If only to get out of the house a few hours every day? Anyhow, once we have the messages home, she wants to go into Boston to Filene's. To get a couple of outfits for work. I'm restless as ever on a weekend, so I tell her I'll ride with her as far as Park Street, for something to do. She looks at me oddly, then just laughs. So we walk up to the Central Square subway station. Buy our tokens at the booth where JoJo Boyle used to sit, making change. Killing time and injuring himself.

We chat a bit on the train, stopping to stare at the Charles and the Boston skyline, where the train comes above ground after Kendall Square. Lucy always loved when the train came out of the tunnel as a child. And I still get a kick out of it, truth to tell. I've always been a public transport man, I suppose. Pleading with the mother to take us upstairs on the double-deckers when we were kids. Which, God love her, she almost always did, giving out how tired she was from town. My brother Jack even ended up a bus conductor, for which I envied him at first. And it would still beat collecting fares on the T. Cooped up in a booth, like what did JoJo's head in.

Meantime I make my living from servicing other people's private transport. Just because you're born in a stable, though, doesn't mean you have to ride a thoroughbred. Which is to say I've never bought a brand-new car. Buying new is a codology, as I told Lucy last year, when she was talking of doing so. The minute you drive it off the lot, you're out of pocket by a couple of thousand. Which is what a new car depreciates, I told her, before the ink dries on your auto loan. We're driving a ten-year-old Toyota these last five years, that does us just fine. It's hard to beat the Jap cars, for all the hoopla about buying American. Even Sal knew better than to drive a Fiat, Italian roots or not. "FIAT," I'd slag him, "Fix It Again Tomorrow!" China has the right idea no doubt, with everybody on a bike. Same as it was in Dublin growing up. Fintan, of course, loves to go on about how the auto has America fucked. And how the big oil lobby won't allow Congress to spend any money on public transport. He's got most of that right, too, I suspect, even if the private auto is what butters our bread. Which makes me, I guess, something like the butcher in one of Lucy's picture books? The one who hated meats? Louis the butcher, who had nightmares of being mugged by pork chops.

I get off with Maggie at Park Street, where I hop the Green Line trolley to the Blue Line for Revere Beach again. The subway cars on the Blue Line are smaller and older. Two benches run along either side, not seats this way and that, like on the Red Line. The passengers look different, too, and I study that up for a while. More beaten down, I decide, as if they have to work harder just to get by. No students either. Across from me is a girl, about fifteen, in a short-sleeved yellow shirt and jeans. With what looks like a brother, a couple of years younger, seated next to her. She's staring out the window, while the lad, who's not quite right, bites his lip, and smiles to himself. I look elsewhere then, as I don't want to seem like I'm staring at a young girl the wrong way. Like I'm a *viejo verde*, eggman or not.

Revere Beach itself looks kind of subdued under the grey sky. As if it too knows the summer is ending. Still, I see where some of the residents in the big nursing home at the corner of the strip have been wheeled out into the carpark. For the fresh air off the ocean. "That home is where I want to end up," Sal used to say. "Overlooking America's oldest public beach." Sal always had great time for Revere, like his family had always lived there. Instead of his father, Enrico LoPresti, having had to flee Brooklyn for Revere, with the INS on his tail. It happened Sal died in an East Cambridge nursing home, however, not Revere. Where his kids put him when his health failed, a few years after I bought the garage off him in 1975.

Kelly's Roast Beef & Clams is open as always, and damned if I don't recognize the 1970 Plymouth Inn in the car park. What's more, your man must have finally gotten round to his spring-cleaning, because there's not half the tins and rubbish in it. The smell's not much better though, given the muggy day. "Would you get me an order of fried clams, buddy?" the guy asks, after we talk for a bit. Poking three dollar bills out the window.

"Lunch is on me," I laugh, and I walk over and get him the clams.

"How's that Irish kid?" he asks when I bring them back. Making me wonder if after thirty years I'm now passing for a Yank, compared to Fintan?

I carry on down the beach then, past the merry-go-round which is now some kind of arcade. It sounds like the same music playing, only there are pinball machines among the ponies, their lights winking, and I just keep walking. I see a lot of the old houses across from the beach are gone. Replaced by high-rise condos, two of which have huge vacancy signs. Probably the smell off the seaweed, which is one thing that hasn't changed about the beach.

Coming back, I see the girl in the yellow shirt from the subway. Seated behind the counter of a balloons & darts game, one of the few remaining amusements along the strip. She's still staring off into space, while the brother, who she must mind even while working, stands twitching in a nearby doorway. It doesn't look anything like the lark Maggie had, working here. Whatever buzz the Beach had in 1959 is long gone this afternoon, and I'm happy just to head back home.

As it happened, Fintan not only showed up to work the Saturday I went out to Revere, but he's largely back to himself over the rest of September. Back to playing ringmaster in the circus that never closes on our corner. Where I'm happy just to have a ringside seat. Looking on and looking back being what I do best. Seeing Fintan, just this morning, pulling some skinny dipso out of the street. Propping him up inside the phone booth on the corner. "I told him to wait till the wind shifts," Fintan laughs.

He's full of horseshit again, too. Like this afternoon, when he starts giving out again about the names for cars. "Skylarks and Cougars, as if your car actually sets you free!"

"Impalas, Mustangs, and Falcons," I name a few models from before his time in America. Just to keep him amped.

"Driving your Cutlass," he snorts, "like you're some class of pirate. A pirate with monthly payments."

"They get it wrong, sometimes," I say. Remembering what my one-time mechanic Rafael remarked about the Chevy Nova. "*No va*" which translates as "it doesn't move", south of the Border. Where GM couldn't shift them for love or money.

"You learning Spanish?" Fintan asks.

"Sure, half the Masses at St Mary's are already in Spanish," I reply. "Demographics," I add, another two-bit word I learned off him.

"You forgot the Barracuda," Lionel says, looking up from an old *Sports Illustrated.* "Which you wouldn't forget, if you met one swimming."

A WEEK LATER Fintan disappears. It's early October, and the sunflowers on Magazine Street are beginning to wither. Half the seeds in their big heads already gone to the birds. A few bums sit mornings in the laundromat next to the Buffet on Prospect Street, soaking up the heat from the dryers. Reminding me of those snakes on a programme of Maggie's, warming themselves on rocks after the sun goes down. That Monday, anyhow, I arrive at work to find a note from Fintan in the till. Saying he'll be back in a few weeks. There's also about forty dollars missing, but I owe him that much easy for overtime. Besides, money's definitely not what Fintan's about.

That afternoon Lionel tells me of some credit-card scam Fintan was on to. Where you pay this party in the MasterCharge billing office fifty bucks, who then tears up your charge slip when it comes in. "Fintan's gonna fly to Bermuda that way," Lionel explains. "Birds fly south for winter," I say, though I doubt Fintan owns any plastic to begin with.

I'm replacing a brake-light bulb in a Nissan an hour later, when I hear my own words fed back to me. "Birds fly south for winter, Darling," only this time they're coming out of the radio, some female singer with a sultry voice and a nice jazzy arrangement behind her. That kind of coincidence is bound to happen, provided you keep eyes and ears open. But it's a good one all the same. Migratory birds and migrant workers, all of them just passing through.

It's funny how quickly Fintan is missed at the garage though. Mrs Casey and Mrs Fitzgerald are both asking after him, and the various Apostles aren't slow either at sussing their main man has moved on. Lionel cracks a joke one afternoon about how the Bermuda Triangle won't be the same, should it swallow Fintan up. But I think you'd have to have your ducks in a row, to get yourself to the Bahamas. Whereas if Fintan's flying south for winter, it's more likely on a Greyhound bound for a cheap motel down in the Keys.

I take the following Saturday off again. Leave the garage with Lionel and this Portagee kid I've taken on part-time to pump gas. It seems a week early for Indian summer — the maples on Magazine Street aren't fully turned — but it's an Indian summer day all right. The sun lovely, once the morning chill is gone. And the sky that particular blue it gets in autumn. Or fall as they say here, which is, for once, the better word.

I give the garden a quick look, then tell Maggie I'm going for a walk. Luis catches me in the front hall going out, however, so I lose a few minutes. Looking at the cistern in their bathroom, which he says is always filling. "Jaysus, you must think I'm your landlord?" I cod Luis. Telling him it needs a new ball cock which I'll sort out later. His English is pretty good — far better than Evangelis' — but I can see he thinks I'm talking dirty by the way he grins.

Finally on my way, I angle up Sydney Street to Mass Ave, and then across the bridge into Boston again. Once I'm over the Charles, I turn east, working my way behind what used to be the Statler Hilton. Past the Combat Zone with its skin flicks and strip clubs. I walk as far down as the financial district around Federal Street, where the office blocks go straight up on all sides, catching the sun at the top. Doubling back then, I end up going into the Arch Street Chapel, of all places.

Where the cool smell of candle wax hits me straight off, though Arch Street is more like a train station than a church. There's Mass on around the clock, plus Confessions, with the faithful perpetually streaming in and out. I kneel down for a while at a pew towards the back, watching the punters come and go. It's mostly old ones at the confessionals, and I marvel I once went to Confession myself. Telling a priest what you got up to with some girl — if you were lucky enough to get up to anything at all. As if it were any of his fucking business to begin with? At least I had copped on to myself by the time Maggie and I became intimate, which was only the year before we married.

"Well, that's my Easter duty done," I think, leaving the chapel. The walking has given me an appetite, so I head into a Waldorf's and order the Daily Special. Clam roll, fries, and coffee. "Red apple!" the counter girl shouts into her mike. Which makes as much sense as the "four toasted blues" the waitress hollered on my first breakfast in America. Only I'm long enough here now to know it was blueberry muffins the crowd behind Sean Hickey and me were ordering.

Anyhow, I puzzle it for a while, till I see on a sign behind her where the Daily Special is called just that: a Red Apple. I count maybe six clams when it arrives, though the few that have snuck into the roll are tasty enough. The fries are thin and mushy, but that's nothing new, if you've been raised on decent chips. You miss all that when you first come over, of course. Crisps instead of potato chips, batch loaf instead of fecking Wonder Bread, never mind proper sausages. Or just apples even: Lambournes, Beauty of Bath or Laxton Superbs. Where here it's mostly three-pound bags of MacIntosh or Golden Delicious at Stop & Shop.

Still you find that some of the Irish never let go. Like the Diamond, who was a terror for getting anyone who went over to bring him back rashers and black pudding. And none of your Dunnes Stores' stuff either. It had to be from this particular Dublin butcher on Dorset Street. Near where he was living in digs after he came up from Kerry. "Don't let on to the Diamond I'm going over!" became the byword in O'Brien's.

"I didn't see any red apple," I joke with the waitress when I pay, only she doesn't get it. Too busy anyhow, flying about the place which is fairly full. Mostly Saturday shoppers, plus a handful of the habitual down-and-outs, slumped over cups of coffee, or maybe a sandwich. It's a bit rich, calling a chain of cut-rate cafeterias after the Waldorf. But then Ritz crackers and Parker House rolls, which you get in the shops, aren't up to much either.

There's no point kidding myself any more about why I've come downtown. So I decide to cut across the Common to the Public Gardens, before walking back down Boylston Street to check out the Hayes Bickford. It's not that I really expect to find Fintan asleep on the grass. Or nursing a coffee midst the other low-rents. But if not, then why am I spending my Saturday like this? It's a good question, even if I can't answer it. I just know I'm trying not to feel pissed off at him. Leaving like he did, not a word said. I know there's no percentage in it, and it's not like I'm his father, either. Though I'll give him an ear-bashing all right, when he comes back.

There's a late-season softball game on the Common, next to Charles Street. Both men and women playing, and maybe a half-dozen spectators. I watch for a few minutes, long enough to figure out the teams are two theatre companies, killing time till show-time. One team is The Pirates of Penzance, at the Colonial, according to a poster. While the other, in Wilbur Theatre tee-shirts, must be doing some comedy, the way they play ball? I cross over to the Public Gardens, where the flower beds are largely finished up. Only the chrysanthemums and asters showing any real colours still, bronzes, yellows, and deep tomato-red. The swan boats are still circling their pond, though their season, too, must be nearly up. I try to remember whether swans fly south, though that's Maggie's department, not mine. Lucy was mad about the swan boats as a kid, and we'd bring her over for a ride every spring. She always said she'd get a job pedalling them, when she grew up, but I guess she meant after spreading her wings in California.

I look around to make sure I don't recognise anybody, before joining the queue at the ticket booth beside the small pier. The boat starts out in its lazy circuit, around the little green house on stilts, and past the tiny island at the other end. The ducks swim over to the boat as always, making me wish I'd brought the Waldorf fries along. "Eat your fill, and pocket none!" as Uncle Derek used to say. When the boat docks, however, I find myself too tired to head down Boylston. "Fuck this for a game of Indians," I decide, as I turn towards Park Street and the subway back to Central Square.

I leave work an hour early that Tuesday, though, and walk over to Fintan's room on Norfolk Street. It rained a cold shower in the morning, but there's a touch of Indian summer again this afternoon. A flock of yellow jackets swarm over the garbage bags outside his tenement. Getting their batteries charged one last time by the sun, before the cold finally finishes them off. There's a puddle in the hallway of his building, directly underneath the cracked skylight at the top of the stairwell. There's a smell of piss also, no doubt stronger after the rain. Plus a host of other odors, as if the damp has activated all the grime that has accumulated through the years.

I get no answer at his door, of course, so I knock up Mrs Lynch on the ground floor. She opens her door in curlers, a thin cardigan over her faded dress, and holding a cigarette. She glares at me until the penny drops. And I get what's probably as close as she ever comes to a smile.

"He left owing two weeks," she says straight off, however. Putting her sourpuss back on, though I'd bet the money matters less than his having left without a word.

"He cleared out his stuff?" I ask.

"Oh, I wouldn't go into his room yet," Mrs Lynch says. "Not until the end of the month." She clearly still has time for Fintan, so. Seeing as she looks the kind who wouldn't be shy about letting herself in, were a lodger even a day late with the rent.

We chat for a bit, standing in the hallway. There's a powerful smell of cat coming from her flat. Which is one way to manage living alone. She tells me her mother was from Clare, though she's never been over. Looking at her, I guess it's probably been hardscrabble enough here, without going back to gawk at the few flinty acres that likely had her mother packing to begin with.

As I leave, she shows me a few scraggly geraniums in the dirt beside the front steps. "Fintan put them in," she tells me. "Leaving me to water them, as if I haven't enough to do." She sounds annoyed, but that's how she always sounds, I reckon.

"He kept the grass picked up, I bet?"

"He did," permitting herself a small smile. "He was very tidy, that way."

"Mr Clean, Neat & Tidy," I laugh at the flowers. "That's our Fintan."

WALKING TO WORK over the next fortnight, I wonder each morning will Fintan be there? There's a real sting in the air now, too sharp for the Haitians who have deserted their lawn chairs beneath the elms on Western Ave. Though maybe it turns out you can't really run the numbers, sitting down? I puzzle that displacement anyhow. From rice fields to city streets is even more of a stretch than from Dublin or a Donegal bog to here. Transplanting is tricky, which is maybe why I was always trying to get Fintan to garden. As if by putting in a few vegetables, he might also put down a few roots?

Lionel still believes Fintan's basking on a Bermuda beach. Keeping himself safe from the barracudas. But I worry that he's more likely sleeping rough somewhere over a hot-air vent. Or else having his own personal Octoberfest, somewhere this side of Munich? An address tag with 'No Fixed Abode' around his neck, as he sleeps it off slumped in a doorway. It would be handy, all the same, had we all labels attached? That stated our fixed abodes? Sort out the homeless problem, so it would. And save those from emigrating, who maybe should stay put? Like Sean Hickey, for one. Who's probably by now also sleeping rough, if he's even still going. Though I understand it's worse for any Irish down-and-out in London. Like the Diamond's brother, who hasn't been heard from in twenty years. Home is where the heart is, unless your heart isn't in it. I remember Sean slipping on a kerb in Boston, those first weeks we were looking for work, and ending up flat on his arse. "Feck it," he said, like he was fighting back tears. "I wish I was at home."

I know it's not Ireland where Fintan's gone to, anyhow. Though he surprised me one morning, not long before he took off. "You could've knocked me over with a feather," he said, describing a truck he saw on Broadway while walking to work.

"An old green Ford pickup, with the roundy kind of cab? I'm already staring at it, when I see LOUGH SWILLY REMOVALS, hand-painted on the door. I chased it half a block, but the light turned green at Columbia, and I couldn't catch it."

That was as near as I ever heard Fintan get to homesick. Even if Lough Swilly is the other end of Donegal from his home place. "I won't go back till they build a bridge," JoJo Boyle used to say. Nor has he, though he used to talk of Sligo once he got tight. And Aunt Kate was nearly as reluctant. Fintan, however, has gone back once since he came over. The summer before last, when he was flush from working for a big trucking outfit in Arizona.

"I was going to do the returned Yank," he told me. "New clothes, big hired car. Buying rounds for anyone with a mouth on them."

But it seemed he shed those notions the moment he went in the door at home. Where he had found his old man, seated at the kitchen table, eating a pitch-black herring which he had roasted on the tongs. Plus a big feed of spuds, the skins piled up on the sheet of newspaper he was using for a plate.

"There was a pile of coal on the kitchen floor behind him. With a black cat pissing on it as I walked in. My father said he nearly choked, seeing me at the door. I nearly choked myself, only I didn't tell him that. An hour passed, and I wanted to be finished with that cottage forever."

That was one of the few times Fintan mentioned Donegal. And maybe the only time he ever mentioned his Da? "Our fathers fuck us up," he used to say a lot, claiming it was from some poem. "Poetry, my arse," I'd tell him. Least not the poetry they beat into us at school. Like I said, people here spend a lifetime blaming their parents for what they did, or didn't, do. Instead of simply getting on with it. Funny enough, though, I didn't tell Fintan, the day he was doing the crossword, the entire story about the birds out back.

About how my father gave them up after his first heart attack. I was working as a kitchen porter in the Gresham, a year or so before I left for the States. Anyhow, I came home that evening to find my mother in bits at the kitchen table. It's funny how little details can fix themselves in your head at a time like that. Like a photograph or something, in which I can still see the Jacobs cream crackers packet next to the Arklow ashtray. Where my mother was stubbing out her Woodbine, her eyes red from crying. "Your father's after being taken into the Mater," she said.

He was a month in bed at home, once he got out of hospital. With herself worn out carrying cups of tea upstairs to him. I

111

was looking after the birds for those weeks, though I was only slinging the seed into them. And trying to remember to give them water. Birds weren't my thing — as if your father's things are ever your own? Anyhow, the day he was strong enough to go out back, all hell broke loose. It wasn't often he lost the head, but it happened that day. "I thought they were being looked after," he bellowed. "Shite and feathers all over the cages!"

"None of them died, did they?" I had pointed out. Not paying him much heed. Nor did it bother me much when he gave them up shortly after. Though my mother was always at him to take them up again. It was only after I came back from America for his funeral three years later, that I felt badly over it. Seeing that bush full of birds in Sutton Cemetery. Which is a bare enough looking place, even in summer. My mother showed me these bird books he'd ordered from England, so he was at least reading about them again.

It was also not until the funeral in 1959, that I realised I had already left Ireland for good. I wasn't that long out then. Hadn't met Maggie yet, and not at all sure about staying on. Not that you're always thinking long-term when you're young. Or at least I wasn't. And no better place than America back then, to allow you go from day to day. The place awash with work, and if you didn't like your job, there was always a better one across the street. Like the yarn Uncle Derek told, about the two lads who heard the streets of New York were paved with gold. They take the boat over, and walking off the pier, one of them spots a fiver on the pavement. He goes to lift it, then stops and turns to his mate, "Sure, I won't start work till tomorrow!"

Back for my Da's funeral, I got reminded how different it was in Dublin. Where the long view was the only option.

Permanent & pensionable if you could get it, but few were that lucky. My brother Jack wasn't on the buses yet. Working instead as the early man in a pub down by the market in Smithfield. My sister, Lizzie, shop assistant in Arnott's wool department, sat in knitting every week-night. The funeral, and the fact it was February, probably made it seem grimmer than it was. But when I flew back to Boston a week later, I knew that time I was leaving Ireland.

It's different here in the States thirty years on, of course. The papers tell you there's all kinds of money being made. But if you study it up, it's not hard to see it's money making money. House of cards stuff, which doesn't last forever. Certainly nothing much is manufactured in America any more — cars, steel, clothes, or shoes. It's all made elsewhere, like Fintan was always ranting. Our Lucy was smart to go into computers, where the jobs are. Even if the computers themselves are all imported.

Which is not to say, of course, that it doesn't change everywhere. Like the single-driver buses in Dublin, which have Jack, the conductor, looking at an early retirement package. Which is gas itself, when you consider early retirement packages aren't even on offer over here. Not unless you're a company president or chairman of the board. How they pull it off at home beats me? Free health care, longer holidays, or dole at the drop of a hat. And all on a pissy economy that wouldn't cover General Motors' telephone bill. Were I twenty-five now, I'd think twice about coming over here at all.

I'm sixty next month, however, and I know I'm not shifting anywhere. Even if they're mad for moving about in this country. Whether it's the sheer size of the place, or everybody behind a wheel, and highways everywhere? Half the population in motion at any given moment, like it were a virus or something. Your man I saw out in Revere, living in his Plymouth, is maybe the most American of all? Even our Lucy, moving out to the West Coast, like she were moving across the street. Or the fellow in this beat-up Olds, who came in needing a universal joint yesterday. He looked nearly my age, yet there he was, having driven clear across the country. From Oregon to here, where he hopes to get a berth as cook on a scalloper out of Chatham, skippered by some guy he knows.

Of course, the Irish are as bad for never staying put. Not just Fintan, but your man in *The Big Wheel of Life* which Fintan lent me, flitting from Scotland to Montana to the Yukon. Or Uncle Derek, who left Ireland more times than he had hot meals growing up. Small wonder he had such time for the travellers, seeing how much he did himself. Though maybe it's just human nature, to want to wander? The grass never green enough in your own back garden?

Anyhow, I'm wondering about Fintan still, as I walk into work the day before Halloween. And someone else comes by looking for him that afternoon. Only she calls him Finny, a young black woman around twenty-five maybe? She's pretty too, in jeans and a purple sweatshirt under this New York Yankees warm-up jacket. Black eye-liner which makes her look a little Chinese. And her hair in what Maggie used to call a bouffant, if that's the word?

"Just tell him Jackie was asking," she says, after I say we haven't seen him in nearly a month.

I don't remember Fintan ever talking about a Jackie either. But I say she seems like a nice girl to Lionel.

"Heart of gold, too," he laughs, shaking his head at me.

"How's that?" I ask, not following.

"You know, Mickey? Like a whore with...?"

"She's on the game?" I sound amazed.

"You got that right," Lionel laughs again. "And it ain't baseball for the Yankees either."

I nearly ask Lionel how he knows, but I'm feeling foolish enough already. Besides, Lionel talked with Fintan in ways I never did, and it's none of my business, anyhow. Though I figure it would be like Fintan, to fall for a hooker among the nighthawks at Hayes Bickford?

WINTER

IT TURNS bitter halfway through November, like winter can't hold itself back. We put a sign out, advertising a special on antifreeze for any radiator we flush. Hoping to bring in maybe an extra punter or two. I hate seeing it so cold this early, as it takes a while to adjust to the change in season. For example, any gas you spill on your hands at the pumps evaporates, drying the skin. In summer that actually feels good, cools them off. But in cold weather the gas makes the skin crack. Which then stings like a bitch when more gas spills on them. You don't keep warm either. Even working on a car in the bays, because you have to keep the doors open, on account of the exhaust. All of which explains, I guess, why Fintan kept moaning about winter before it even arrived. He wasn't the first worker I've lost to the cold either, and I have my eye on Lionel now. To see is he going to stick it. And so far, so good.

"You lose seventy-five per cent of your body heat through your head," I cod him one morning, when he's pissing about the wind-chill factor. "And that's with hair on it!"

"Yeah, and seventy-five per cent of human communication is nonverbal," he smiles, flipping me the finger. I notice he comes in the next day, though, with a blue woolen watch cap on. Looking like a warmer middleweight. "You can't have hair and brains both," I console him, quoting Uncle Derek.

At home I bring in the couple of pumpkins I've grown every year since Lucy was a kid. She used to carve up the largest for a jack o' lantern. Though we stopped putting it out on the porch, after it got smashed one year. We don't carve them anymore, but Maggie will make pumpkin pie for

Thanksgiving. I also throw another layer of straw on the asparagus bed, after we get four nights straight of a hard ground frost. Which pretty much kills off every last thing in the garden. I know you can grow cabbage through the winter in Ireland, but then you can't grow asparagus over there. Or at least I don't think you can? It took me a while to get the hang of asparagus when I first dug the bed. The trick is to dig it deep enough, then throw enough manure in to feed it for years, since you can't disturb the soil once it roots. In short, you have to get it precisely right at the start. And even then you have to wait three years before you get a crop to eat. Still, there's something magical about asparagus, coming up, year after year, in the same spot. Waving their green feathery heads, like they know they have all the other vegetables beat. I often wonder what makes your pee smell so, after a feed of them, but that's not the kind of thing they bother with in gardening books.

There's a dusting of snow over Thanksgiving, and suddenly it's December before you know it. I'm noticing not many Apostles call in anymore. Though Mario Andretti drove by yesterday on metal rims, the rubber gone off his wheelchair. Lionel is a demon for rotating tires. "I've seen more tread on newspaper," he's always telling customers about a bald tire. Rotating it with their spare, if he can't sell them one of the retreads we stock. But there's nothing he can do for the wheels under Mario. Who looks even grubbier than usual, unshaven, with a threaded lump on his brow. Lionel chats with him a bit, though. Then slips him a bill from his wallet, when he thinks I'm not looking. From what Fintan said, Mario lives in a plywood box between two tenements over on Columbia, however he manages to keep warm in the dead of winter. Not to mention the guy living in his Plymouth

Inn. Only I guess it's a Lincoln Inn now? After he pulled in last week in a 1972 Lincoln-Continental, its back seat piled high with blankets and old coats.

It's a funny thing, but I find myself now taking in the derelicts throughout Central Square. Like these two winos slumped yesterday against Libby's Liquors on Mass Ave. The mouth on the taller one opening and closing like a fish out of water, beached by a receding tide. Or John the Baptist, the looney-tune with the ginger hair and green stocking cap. Talking to himself outside the Buffet last week, though I didn't see any sign of his fiddle. I'm also noticing the other transplants I've taken for granted over thirty years. Stopping only today to stare at four Chinese enjoying a burst of weak December sun on a bench at the top of Magazine Street, the eldest cutting the others' hair.

The other funny thing, of course, is me and Lionel. Who's easy enough with me to be flipping me the bird. And visa-versa, I suppose. He's also working me hard to take on his cousin, Beetle. Another ace mechanic, he swears. I can't imagine hiring somebody named Beetle, however. Even if I'd have laughed ten years ago at the idea of taking on an Irish with an earring. Or a coloured of any stripe, never mind a tattooed baldy one, sporting coconut perfume. Still, Beetle or no Beetle, our turnover barely covers carrying two mechanics full-time. So now that Fintan has split, I'm better off hiring a kid part-time to pump gas, while Lionel and I handle the repairs. Even so, Evangelis' mother came by last week, wondering would I take the Karate Kid back on? It seems all E-Man does is fight with his father at their pizza place, off Inman Square. I told her No Can Do, but we chatted for a couple of minutes. Mrs Kapopoulos told me they were fed up with America, and planned to sell up and move back to

Greece. Lock, stock and barrels of money, no doubt. The Greeks are like the Portagees, working two jobs at a go. Or starting up a sub shop, where the entire family works unwaged, saving every penny.

"Broken glass everywhere you walk," Mrs Kapopoulos said. Struggling to explain her disappointment with the Land of Opportunity. Of course, once she said that, I'm noticing bits of glass all around for days after. Until we get our first real snowfall of the year. Though there's less broken glass, I think, ever since the Legislature passed the bottle bill, giving you a nickel deposit back. Or a couple of bucks for entrepreneurs like the Philosopher, who pushed a shopping cart of returnables past the garage just last week. Land of Opportunity how are ye!

LUCY ONLY GETS a couple of days at Christmas, so Maggie has decided to fly out to spend the week with her. She's happy at having saved enough from her job at Corcoran's for her ticket, though she's feeling badly about leaving me for the holiday.

"Will you be all right, Mickey?" she asks.

"I'll struggle on," I tell her, though in fact it suits me fine. Christmas is for when you're a child — or for when Lucy was — but it's not my favourite time of year. My mother used to wear herself out getting ready for it when we were kids. Though we took no notice of that, then. Still, it was a nice day at home. Ham for the dinner, and a walk along the Bull Wall if the weather was anyways nice. Even my father along, though Jack and I couldn't wait to get back home to play with whatever toy Santy brought. I remember the Christmas I got a toy train. And the Christmas Jack got a secondhand melodeon, and woke the house at four a.m., trying to play it. Though most years we got only a stocking with some fruit and maybe a bar of chocolate.

"You'll go over to Patti's for your dinner?"

"Either that," I tease, "or the Christmas buffet at the Buffet." Though all that kip offers by way of food is some warmed-up cocktail sausages during Happy Hour.

"You'll take it easy, won't you?" Maggie says, looking worried now.

"Just enough to keep the rust off," I reassure her.

I take it easy though, all the same. Maybe not having to bang on the pipes from my basement easy chair takes the edge off the odd pop. Or maybe I'm finally smart enough not to slip my traces, simply cause Maggie's not around. I like having the house to myself, no doubt about it. Even if things have been easier between us the last few months. Maggie is happier in herself, ever since she started at Corcoran's. As if simply getting out of the house was half of what she needed. Though Lucy would eat me if I made a comment like that. It's gotten so you can pass no remarks on women whatsoever. At least not in front of the younger ones.

In any case, there's been less small-arms fire at home for some time now. We've even been intimate twice in the past month. What the sportscasters might call "a personal best", given our track record in that department of late? It also helps that Lucy's taken to calling home each week, which perks Maggie up no end. Mother and child are wired differently to father and child, that's for sure. Never mind how fathers and mothers are wired — or what it really comes down to — men and women. You'd want to be an electrician to read those schematics, so you would. Or maybe it's different kinds of trees, as I was thinking the other night, looking at this TV programme with Maggie. Thinking that men were like conifers: more upright, uptight even. And staying the one way year-round. While women are more like deciduous trees. More open, spreading out, not afraid to shed their leaves or tears. Though it's probably more a matter of fish and fowl. Or creatures from two different planets altogether.

"Can you figure out women?" JoJo used to ask, when he was having trouble with the wife.

"Can you *what?*" I'd ask him back. Not in this lifetime, John Paul.

On Christmas morning I give Guzzles a tin of salmon for a treat, before heading out to the sister-in-law Patti's house, like I promised Maggie. Luis and Fatima had asked me down when they heard Maggie was to be away, but I said I was already taken care of. There's no time like Christmas for a family row, and opting for turkey with the tenants over the in-laws sounds a likely recipe. Besides, while I like Luis and Fatima, I'm not sure Portagees don't eat something like eel for their Christmas dinner? And while Maggie has me eating garlic and rosemary on roast potatoes now, I'm not yet ready for eel with stuffing and cranberry sauce. Though whatever they're having smells tasty as I pass their door downstairs in the front hall.

Coming out of the house, I see a crutch lying in the front yard. Just inside the chain-link fence, next to an empty can of Colt 45. It's a wooden one, with a red-foam cushion for your armpit, as opposed to the aluminum jobs which clasp your upper arm. Nothing remarkable, only it looks somewhat strange lying there. Where it wasn't lying fifteen minutes earlier, when I came back from the shop with the *Globe*. I stare at it for a moment, like it's a clue to some puzzle I'm working on. Next thing I know, I'm wondering how — and where — Fintan is spending his Christmas day.

I'm past being cheesed off at his leaving like he did. But I still miss the crack from having him around. All his bullshit, plus the stories and yarns. Though to be honest, stories were most of what we swapped. Either that, or simply shooting the breeze. When Fintan wasn't running his mouth about the state of the cosmos, that is. It's not like we often ever said anything to one other. And if I could never quite puzzle him out, Christ knows what he made of me. Not that there's any great mystery involved.

I prop the crutch up against the fence, like you do some kid's mitten you find on the snow. Though you'd miss a crutch sooner than a mitten, limping along on one wing. Unless, seeing it's his birthday, Christ is parceling out a few miraculous cures this morning? Either that, or Colt 45 is powerful stuff altogether. I wouldn't fancy being on crutches in winter, in any case. Least of all on Christmas Day, trying to cross Western Ave towards Putnam Square and my dinner. I remember having them for a sprained ankle one autumn years ago. And realising how something like that reshapes your entire life. Like having to find a seat as near as possible to the subway train door. Or avoiding wet leaves when it rains. The best, though, was the evening I cut down the alleyway in the Square beside the steak house. To meet Maggie, who was waiting in the carpark. I had on this long overcoat I had got years before. For fifteen bucks, secondhand in the Salvation Army shop. Though it must have easily cost a couple of hundred new. Maggie had been after me to get rid of it for ages. "Your hobo coat," she called it, only there was great warmth in it from the tweed. Anyway, the moment I came out the alley, coat flapping and crutches flying, these three bums at the back of the carpark started hustling in my direction. Three more scarecrows, having mistook me for one of their flock, and only hoping I'd be carrying a fresh pint of Flame Tokay besides. There but for the Grace of God, like the man said. "Maybe you'll get rid of that coat now?" Maggie laughed, having eyed the pantomime from the car.

It's funny the look into other lives that something as simple as being on crutches gives you. Instead of being all wrapped up in your own world, like it's the only one going? Or maybe it's Christmas Day that gets you thinking that way. Anyhow, I remember that Saturday last October, coming back from the swan boats, after going into Boston to look for Fintan. Passing this couple on the Common, the guy holding his wife's arm, who was herself holding a white stick. Crutches are one thing, I remember thinking, but there was another reality altogether. Thinking how different those two lives must be, day to day. And thinking — for the brief moment such thoughts last before you slip back into your own life — of how many different lives there are. Mario Andretti's, say, to my Uncle Derek's? Or Lionel's to JoJo's, whatever about my own?

I eat too much Christmas dinner, same as I would do at home. Patti's Joe doesn't take a drink, but Patti looks after me with sherry before the meal. And wine during, and some Jack Daniels afterwards. I pretend to be interested in the first half of some Bowl game on TV, before I make my excuses and head home. Though in-laws are a piece of cake, I find, compared to your own family. And family's not so bad, provided you can keep an ocean in between. Aunt Kate was as much as I've had over here, and Aunt Kate was all right besides.

It's clear and cold, just like you'd expect at Christmas, with a first-quarter moon in the darkening sky. There's not much traffic out, either, as I make my way back along Green Street past the police station. Cutting across the lower part of the Square, I find myself once more thinking about Fintan. Or I'm remembering rather, an evening last August when he and I went out to the dogs in Revere. Same Blue Line, only you get off at Wonderland. Which is a great name for a dog track, I have to admit. Coaxing the punters back, no matter how much they lost their previous outing. Like the old codger who queued to bet in front of us, hands shaking as he studied the racing form.

Still, the track was something of a wonderland. Not the indoor part with its green benches in front of a row of TV monitors, but the track itself. Walking out to it, I was almost startled by how green the infield grass looked, lit by these towers of blazing arc lamps. I had said as much at the time to Fintan, who remarked that Fenway Park at night looks the same. And that we should take in the Sox again. We never got back to the ballpark, nor did we do the dog track again. Even though I made seventy bucks on the Trifecta with a blind bet that night. The dogs, chasing a mechanical rabbit, weren't a patch on a horse race however. All that thunder, and dirt flying up from their hooves, as they come down the homestretch. Not that I'm much for the ponies, either. Unlike my brother Jack, who has a path worn from his local to the bookie across the road .

After the last race, I had told Fintan I would buy him a drink with my winnings. I was tempted to hop the Blue Line, take him down to the bar at the Beach where I had once worked.

But we went into this neighbourhood place, not far from the track, instead. "You should save that payoff for your retirement," Fintan said when I ordered us a second beer. I told him then about Hardy. Hardy, a six-foot-six German with a shaved head like Lionel's, who worked this Copley Square building site with Sean Hickey and me the year we came over. The night the job finished up, we were all drinking in the South End. However, when I went to buy one for Hardy, who was going back to Hamburg, he held up a hand the size of a ham.

"You put money away, Mickey," he said. In this gas German accent, down deep, like he's beating on a drum. "Some day you have none, and be hungry. You put hand in pocket, find money for a sandwich. You think of Hardy, then, and have a drink!"

Fintan laughed, looking across the booth at me. "You know a thing or two, Mickey. You know it's all in the moments anyhow."

"I know it's not running in circles after a clockwork hare," I said. "Whatever it is." Not that I don't head out every morning with my egg basket, same as the rest. But life's what you find in front of you every day. Not farther down the road, nor over the rainbow.

Looking back now as I walk home on Christmas night, I wonder are those few words as much as we truly ever said to one another? As if, despite everything else, we were alike that way? One spider knowing another, like I said already.

It's business as usual the day after Christmas here, unlike Ireland which pretty much shuts down for the week. At work, Lionel says he and Diane are staying in New Year's Eve. In case I want to come over and watch the Times Square bit on

TV. I make some excuse, thanking him all the same. Easy as it's become at work, I'd be like a Jew in jail, all nerves, if I were seated in their sitting-room. So I spend the night at home instead. Looking at this book on Irish gardens Maggie got me for the Christmas.

She's in good form when she comes back from seeing Lucy. What's more, the pair of them are planning a trip to Ireland in June. And Maggie's trying to get me to sign up for this tour of Irish Gardens, which would take me over at the same time, too.

"You must be joking," I tell her, looking at the brochure with its photo of Powerscourt where I cycled once. And a slew of other big houses I never heard of. Though I recognise a couple from the book she gave me. "Mickey the Mechanic joins the blue-rinse brigades?"

"There'll be other men along."

"Yeah, doctors and lawyers," I say, not wanting to start a fight. The gardens look all right though. Some with trees brought back from China in the nineteenth century, plus other exotic stuff. "Leave it with me for a while," I add, though I've no intention of signing up.

IF MAGGIE IS happy working, I'm fed up through all of January into early February. It's partly the winter, I know, which feels like it'll never end. We haven't seen much snow, but we didn't get a January thaw, either. So what snow has fallen lies there yet, all dirty grey from the traffic. The ice on footpaths where people failed to shovel is grey too. And rock-hard, making it treacherous underfoot. I mind where I step, walking into work. Maggie bought me these straps with steel prongs that slip over your boots. Giving you a purchase on the ice like mountaineers is the idea, I suppose. Like the chains for your tires in winter, before snow tires came in. I admit I laughed when Maggie gave me them. But I'm using them now, if the going's especially slick, not wanting to risk a fall at my age.

Funny enough, the crossword has an eight-letter blank for the spikes on a climber's boots the first morning I wear them into work. Which is the kind of coincidence I like. Only Fintan, who had most of the answers, isn't on hand, and Lionel just laughs when I ask him. Though he later tells me a quick one about this passenger giving out in the *Titanic* bar: "I know I asked for ice in my drink, but this is ridiculous!"

It's not just winter that has me down, however. Not the morning I arrive to see somebody's kicked in the corner phone booth again. Bits of glass lying everywhere, reminding me of Mrs Kapopoulos, who's heading back to Greece. Mornings like this, I feel like packing in the job myself, which isn't getting any easier. Not yesterday anyhow, when we had a big barney with this Jamaican. Who drives in a Chevy Caprice, billows of blue smoke trailing out the tailpipe.

"You need more than a tune-up," I tell him straight off. "Some internal problem there."

"Tune-up's all I want, mon," he tells me in that gas West-Indian accent.

"You're the boss," I tell him, so Lionel tunes it up. Of course, the car's still blowing smoke when he starts it up, and the Jamaican announces he's not paying. I'm too tired to fuck around, so I tell him of Massachusetts General Law, Chapter 186, Section 15(B). Which gives me, Mickey McKenna, of

423 Prospect Ave, Cambridge, Massachusetts, an automatic mechanic's lien on any vehicle with an unpaid bill.

"Fuck you, mon," the Jamaican says. Which suggests I shouldn't give up my day job to become a lawyer. So I call the cops instead, who eventually persuade the Jamaican to pony up, after which they go across to Dunkin Donuts, being cops and all.

It's as much the newer cars though, as the customers, which are wearing me down. Making it harder to do the job right. Once you could see hear or smell half the problems with a car. See it misfiring, for example, on account of a crossed ignition wire. Until ignitions went electronic, that is. Or get a raw gas smell that made your eyes water, if the carburetor hadn't the air-to-fuel ratio right. But fuel injection gets rid of the carburetor, making it harder to diagnose that problem. As in diag-nose? Catalytic converters also compensate for the bad smell you once got with a wrong mixture, giving you less to go with.

Anyhow, once I see the phone booth shattered, I start noticing the litter everywhere. The lumps of dirty ice, the dog shit, the whole nine yards. It's enough to start you thinking of heading off. If not back to Greece or Dublin, at least out of the city? Maybe get a place up in New Hampshire, with half the taxes and room for a massive garden? "The best advice a man can heed: Plant no more garden than your wife can weed." Or so Uncle Derek said, who had neither wife nor garden. While I have both, though Maggie doesn't weed at all. In any case, I doubt I'd like country life any more than I would suburban Arlington. Once a jackeen, never a culchie.

I know the fact Luis and Fatima are moving out is part of what has me antsy. Having saved their down payment, they're buying a house in Union Square, just over the Somerville line. I know losing your tenants is nothing — not even close to having your own daughter move out. Just something else to remind you change is the name of the game. Which is what a garden shows you every day, only there's no bloody gardening in February. Which only feeds the lousy feeling. Still, I don't mention Luis and Fatima's moving out at work. Lionel has a newly married nephew who's looking to rent, and I figure I'm not there yet, either.

THEN, ON THE last Saturday in February, we get held up. Or Lionel does, as I'd left early to take Maggie up to Sears in Porter Square. To choose the colour she wants for the front hall, which I'm promising to paint before spring comes, and I'm back out in the garden. What's more, Lionel gets knifed by one of two coloureds who come in just as he's closing up, looking for whatever's in the till. The cop who phones me at home, after Maggie and I get back, tells me Lionel got cut pretty bad. But it's not life-threatening, or anything like that. "No vital organs," says the cop.

I ring Lionel's Diane, then go up to check on the garage that evening. Even though the cop said Lionel had them secure it, while they're waiting on the ambulance. Everything looks in order when I get there, right enough. When I step behind the counter, however, I see blood all over the floor. Plus a big wad of bloody paper toweling, off the roll for cleaning windscreens, stuffed in beside the till. There's blood on the phone, too, where Lionel must've dialled 911 after he got stuck. Then propped himself between counter and window, till the cruiser arrived.

It snows heavy that night. Coming down for hours in big lazy flakes, with hardly any wind. It's funny how quiet a snowstorm makes the street. You have fewer cars out, and those that are out take it easy, their tires muffled by the snow on the road. It's absolutely beautiful the next morning. Like a wonderland, only not a greyhound in sight. There must be nine or ten inches of the stuff. Blanketing everything: parked cars, sidewalks, hedges, the whole world outside. Below our kitchen window, the garden looks like it has a few bodies buried in it, where the snow has humped up on the raised vegetable beds. Even the bird house I got Maggie for her birthday last month has its peaked roof of snow. Propped on its pole like a miniature Swiss chalet or something.

I sit at the kitchen table and ring the hospital to see about visiting hours. "The church, dear," I tell Maggie, when she asks who I'm ringing. "Just in case Mass has been snowed out." Outside, the snow stuck to the maple nearest the house has enlarged its limbs, like the kitchen window were glazed with magnifying glass. I ring Mrs Kapopoulos next. To see would Evangelis come back for however long it takes Lionel to mend. While I'm on the phone, a seagull lands on the snow-covered garage next door. Feathering the air with its wings as it settles, looking for all the world like something blowing on a clothesline.

I shovel off the back and front steps and footpath before setting off. Leaving the driveway until I get back. It's a light puffy snow, not the heavy wet stuff which brings on a heart attack, and I've the job done in twenty minutes. The plows were by early, so I walk in the street, the trees all powdered sugar overhead. It's still grey, the temperature around thirty, I'd guess, with just the slightest breeze blowing. It looks like everybody in the Port is having a lie-in, as only one or two cars pass me along Magazine Street. Everywhere you look is a white blanket of snow. Except for the odd splash of yellow, same bright shade as the lemon slush at Revere Beach, where a dog has lifted its leg. "Don't eat the yellow snow," we used to caution Lucy when she was small. And teased her with, when we knew she knew better.

Central Square is even quieter than usual for a Sunday morning. There are a few people about on foot, but I'm actually able to stand in the middle of Mass Ave for a full minute. Like I'm a traffic cop, admiring the snow on the shopfronts in both directions, a flock of pigeons wheeling overhead in the grey sky. I carry on straight down Prospect, past the laundromat and the Buffet, and the big health-food store which last week Maggie tells me is owned by some Irish guy.

I pick up a few doughnuts for Lionel across from the garage. Pausing only to peer in the office window to see if everything is in order. It is — apart from the red light on the coffee machine. Winking back at me like the tiny lamp in front of the Sacred Heart picture in my parents' bedroom. And you'd want something like a Sacred Heart, to survive that coffee. Staring in, I gauge there's enough in the pot so it won't evaporate and crack. Which is a good thing, as I haven't the keys to the place, anyhow. As I'm standing there, the guy I hire to plow the garage wheels in his truck. So I have a quick word with him, before carrying on up Broadway to the hospital.

Cambridge City Hospital it used to be called. Only I see Cambridge Hospital on the sign in front now. I remember reading something about Harvard taking it over, like a teaching hospital or something. So I figure the name change must be part of that. It's all one-stop shopping now anyhow.

A psychiatric ward on the fourth floor, detox unit on the third, and Lionel in Room 207 on the second floor. Or so they tell me at the information desk inside. It's funny how just walking into a hospital can give you the willies, even if you're only visiting. Like you get slightly edgy all the same. Part of it is the smell, I think. Smiling to myself, as I remember taking Lucy into hospital as a little girl.

"What's that smell, Papa?"

"Something they use to keep it clean, Pet."

"Well, if they keep it clean, how come it smells?" And I hadn't an answer for that.

Lionel's in a room with a guy about my age, whose left foot is in traction. A white guy, who looks at me a bit puzzled. Like maybe wondering why I'm visiting Lionel?

Or maybe I'm putting that on to him, I don't know. Meantime, Lionel's lying halfways propped up on pillows, looking nowhere near his stylish self in a hospital gown.

"What's happening, Mickey?" he lifts a hand off the bedclothes. I didn't know blacks could look pale, but he's definitely washed out, a bit grayish about the face. Though he's hardly black to begin with, surrounded by white sheets and white gown. More like a deep shade of mahogany. Except I doubt his daddy would like it any better, had he to check off "mahogany" on a form?

"I got you these," I hand him the Dunkin Donuts bag. "They were all out of ham on rye."

"Don't make me laugh," he winces, looking into the bag to see what kind I got.

"Sugar crullers," I tell him. "Same as you get every day."

"Have one, Mickey," he holds out the bag.

"Thanks, no," I say. "I eat one of them, it sits in my stomach for a week."

"Everything all right at the garage?" he asks.

"Yeah, except you left the coffee pot on," I cod him.

"Jus' trying to break it," he smiles. "'Fore some customer sues your ass for serving that shit."

We chew the fat like that for a few minutes. Before Lionel pulls up his gown to show me the bandage taped across his belly. "Nineteen stitches," he says.

"You didn't have to get cut up," I tell him, "over what was in the till."

"You're fucking right I didn't!" Lionel snaps. Pissed off like, which puzzles me for a moment? However, he relaxes a bit, then grins.

"I thought I could take the mother," he says, explaining how he tried to knock the knife out of the guy's hand. "Only I guess I'm not as quick as I was."

"It's that sugar cruller every day," I say. "Slows you down."

"Though I pity the poor bastard," I add, "if you'd had a big, big Coke to hand."

"That was jus' some white boy," Lionel smiles. "Wouldn't know how to use a blade anyhow."

We talk for a while more. Till a nurse comes in to change his bandage, and I get up to go.

"Later, Mickey," he lifts his hand again.

"See you in the spring when the bed gives way," I tell him. Which was Uncle Derek's favourite parting shot. "Keep your best foot forward," I tell the guy in traction in the other bed, who has disappeared behind the Sports section of the *Sunday Globe*.

I get in the elevator, but instead of pressing G for Ground, I hit the button for the third floor. "Boyle?" I ask the nurse at the desk, who looks every inch a ward boss. Like she could run Mayor Daly's Chicago, whatever about the Cambridge City detox unit. I see her eyeing me — to see if I'm carrying — before she says, "305," pointing down the floor.

Last week, one of the lads from O'Brien's, in for gas, tells me JoJo's in hospital. After being found in bed, half-dead from too much drink and too little food. It's over a year since I saw him, but even so, I'm not prepared for the sight. Like he's sunk into the bed, an IV feed in an arm that's little more than skin and bone. And the skin itself with this yellowy tinge, like Garrity the eggman.

"How's Mickey?" he says, thanking me for coming in.

"I don't know about you, Boyle," I tell him, "but I'm here for the softball."

"Poor Barney died last Christmas," JoJo says, as I pull a chair up to the bed.

"So what's your hurry?" I want to ask him. Only you can't say that kind of thing. I hadn't heard about Barney O'Sullivan from O'Brien's either, which JoJo sees from my face.

"You haven't been around, Mickey."

"Confined to barracks," I say. Though I know JoJo knows better. JoJo, whose own wife threw him out years ago.

"How's Maggie?" he asks. As if to remind me he was our best man at the wedding. Even if I bailed out on him years ago.

"Ah, she's grand, JoJo," I say, wishing to fuck I'd not come to see him.

"Still calling the shots," he laughs, like he's letting me off the hook anyhow.

After a while a nurse comes in with his lunch on a tray. A bowl of soup and a slice of Wonder bread. I get up to leave, but she tells me to sit tight, all smiles and efficiency. She's lovely too, dark hair under her white cap. Nothing like the battle-axe at the desk, though I've always been a sucker for the uniform. There was a student nurse, May, back in Dublin when I was twenty-two, who I saw for a while. And who, had she felt similarly, might have kept me there? Though I told myself, after it ended, it had been more the uniform than anything else.

"She's promised me a steak," JoJo says, "once I've mended." Like he's apologising for the meagre rations.

"You culchies would talk a dog away from a meat wagon," I tell him.

JoJo tells then how Mrs Diamond has taken to collecting her husband from O'Brien's at ten o'clock, any night the Diamond manages to get in for a scoop.

"Cost-saving measures," I say. Telling JoJo how she finally copped onto the empty oil can last July.

"Did you bring me anything, Mickey?" JoJo asks when I get up to go a while later.

"Was it rashers you wanted?" I ask. "Or black pudding?"

"You've a bottle attached to you, for fuck's sake!" is more what I want to say. Give the IV a tug, in case he's forgotten. But that's only more of what you can't say. Or I can't say anyhow.

"It's Sunday, JoJo," I say instead. "No carry-outs." Though I don't promise him a naggin the next time I'm in either.

I'm not sure there's even a next time in it, I think, crossing Cambridge Street towards home. I had stopped seeing JoJo because I was drinking too much with him. But that wasn't the only reason, I know by now. It wasn't just a matter of letting go of JoJo, or O'Brien's. But of letting go of Ireland also. Like I needed to plant myself, as it were, over here. Or else end up neither here nor there. Beached somewhere in between, like a lot of Irish who come over. The Diamond, for example, still chasing his sausages and white pudding. Or Sean Hickey, drifting like a ghost somewhere down Nighthawk Alley. Or that fellow, seated with his back to the café window, in that very painting? A kind of mystery man, who I used to imagine might be Irish, even if the suit looked too good. Nursing a cup of coffee into the wee hours, like he's wishing he was elsewhere? I don't know you're ever anything but a transplant, away from home. And I know I carry Dublin inside me. The road I grew up on, Dollymount, the family, and so on. Just like JoJo carries Sligo, or the Diamond Dingle, or Fintan Donegal. But some transplants manage to take root elsewhere. When soil conditions — and your luck, I guess — are favourable.

I cut over to Harvard Street, more residential, and nicer to walk along than Broadway. The snow is packed down on the road by now, and folks are beginning to dig out their cars buried by the ploughs. When I get home, I don't feel like going down to the basement. Though that's what I usually do while Maggie puts the Sunday dinner on. I think of offering to set the table. But I can see her offering to take my temperature, if I did that. So I sit down with the *Sunday Globe* in the sitting room instead.

That Tuesday a Detective LaRocca comes by the garage. A burly Italian about fifty, wearing an anorak, or parka as they're called here. "We picked up two Negroes last night," he says. "Pulled a knife on the manager of The White Hen in North Cambridge. Might be the same boys did you on Saturday." Only he sort of sneers when he says "Negroes", like what he means is niggers.

"How long's your boy been working for you?" he asks.

"The kid?" I ask. Pointing out the window at Evangelis, filling up a white Porsche.

"Naw, the boy what got nicked on Saturday," LaRocca says.

"About eight or nine months," I say, as the penny finally drops. "And his nick took twenty stitches."

LaRocca just shrugs. As if to say thieves have been known to fall out among themselves.

"Lionel's sound," I tell him, out straight.

"Then he can pick 'em out of a lineup," he laughs. "They're better at telling each other apart anyhow."

LaRocca fucks off in his brown Ford Fairlane, which, like most unmarked cop cars, you can spot a mile off. Leaving me to suddenly see why Lionel got so shirty in hospital. When I remarked that he needn't have gotten cut up over the money. Like I was implying he'd maybe risked it, so I wouldn't think it had been an inside job? Or a matter of brothers helping brothers out? When I'd have never thought it, before that fat Wop for a cop came by. Though, to be honest, it's the kind of thing I might have wondered — if I didn't know Lionel. So there I am for the next hour, feeling bothered at having thought it. Even though I hadn't thought it, whatever that's about?

We're busier than a Chinese fire drill the next couple of weeks. Till the doctor gives Lionel the green light to work again.

"I'm not supposed to lift anything heavy for a month," he says his first morning back.

"When'd you ever do anything heavy?" I ask, pleased to have him back. Never mind Evangelis having me already driven spare. Still, when E-Man asks can he stay on another fortnight till his family leaves for Athens, I say yes. Figuring it might keep his father from cutting him up into a Greek salad at their pizza joint. "Only you can kung-fu off," I warn him, "if you start banging your head off my bench again."

"*No, gracias,*" I tell this skinny Puerto Rican with a bucket and squeegee that same afternoon, asking do I want the windows washed. *No gracias* being among the half-dozen words I learned off Rafael.

"I could speak four or five languages once," Lionel says after the PR leaves.

"You could in your barney," I tell him.

"Only for one night, man. I was stationed in Mannheim, after 'Nam. Someone had scored this Pakistani hash, and I'm on my bunk, stoned out of my gourd. The only one left in the barracks, cuz the rest have gone down to the beer hall. I'm playing with the dial on this little transistor radio, picking up all these German, French, and Spanish stations. What blows my mind is I'm digging everything! Next think I know, I'm looking eye-to-eye at this mother, standing next to my bunk. Wearing a balaclava, and pointing a Browning at me.

"'Where's the shit?' he says, but I jus' laugh. Thinking it's one of the guys, pretending to rip off the dope for a joke. 'Where's the shit?' he says again, but I'm still laughing, I'm that fucked up. Luckily he sees that fo' himself, so he starts trashing the foot lockers, looking fo' the stuff. I don't pay him no mind, anyways, cuz I'm trying to tune in this Dutch DJ, keeps fading in and out."

It's nice having Lionel back, seeing he tells the odd story too. Like Fintan would. Most of the chat over here is just chat. About sports, or what was on the box last night, including the frigging ads. But Lionel's more like somebody Irish, who actually spins you a yarn. Of course Fintan had a cockeyed theory here, too — about blacks and Irish. "There's a nod you give in Donegal," he told me once. "Just a wee twist of the head at whoever you meet. I've done it for years over here, Mickey, and blacks are the only ones who've ever read it."

"Soul brothers," I mocked, but Fintan insisted there was something to it. "Secret signals, Mickey. One spider knows another."

IT'S PADDY'S DAY next, before you know it. It's a school holiday in Boston too. Though they make out it's to celebrate the Brits getting whipped back in 1776. If they admit it's because of Paddy's Day, they'll have the Italians wanting Padre Pio Day off. Or the Polacks hollering Casmir Pulaski's birthday ought to be made a holiday. Pulaski was this Polish general who helped row George Washington across the Potomac. Or so claimed this big Polack, Zalinski, who worked for me years ago, about the time I took over from Sal. I had tried learning a little Polish off him, to go with my Spanish, only I couldn't get my tongue around it. I'd tell Zalinski a Polish joke, then I'd go up to O'Brien's and tell the same one about a Kerryman. Both Polack and Paddy raised on the same diet: potatoes, Church, and alcohol.

March 17th is just another day for me, however. Though Maggie and I used to take Lucy into Southie for the parade when she was little. It was a gas parade back then. Rows of schoolgirls marching in Aran knits and Kelly-green skirts. Some with tall green feathers, like asparagus plants, on their heads. Waving batons and doing cartwheels. You could imagine them clearing the streets of most Irish villages back then, strutting their stuff. I haven't seen the Southie parade in nearly fifteen years. Not since the time JoJo and I ran into Sean Hickey with his cut-up face. But I understand the Dublin parade has jazzed itself up since. No longer just the postal vans and army lorries with a couple of pipe bands.

What's different about this Paddy's Day is that I end up drinking after work with Lionel. Drowning the shamrock in a coloured bar on River Street. Most days Lionel drives his Buick Electra to work, but he'd loaned it to his son that morning. So we're walking home together, up Prospect, when he asks do I want a beer?

I say sure, figuring he means Ken's on Mass Ave. A big place with whites and coloureds both.

"High time you saw Porky's Place," he laughs instead. Like he's got me now. I'm tight as a drum going in, but Lionel just waves at Porky, who's as thin as a rail. The place is about the size of the Buffet, only it seems darker inside. Which makes the coloured lights over the rows of bottles behind the bar seem brighter, if that makes any sense? As we slip into a booth, I glance around quick to see can I spot another white guy. When I look back at Lionel, he just smiles. As if to say, "Relax, man, you're just the token honky."

"My treat, Mickey," is what he actually says. Waving away my money when I try to pay for two long-neck bottles of Schlitz. After which this old black guy, all wrinkles and tight grey curls, comes over to our booth, wearing a suit nearly as creased as his face.

"How you doing?" he says to me, before turning toward Lionel. They chat for a minute, before the guy turns to go back to his stool.

"You still playing?" Lionel asks.

"You see a piano in my back pocket?" the old guy laughs, which gives him another million wrinkles. I'm trying to gauge how old he is, somewhere between sixty-five and six hundred.

"How's your father keeping?" I ask Lionel, who rolls his eyes at the question.

"He's this dog, Flash, about as old as he is, dying from a half-dozen different things. So I take him and Flash into Angel Memorial last week, to get the dog put down. Just standing at a counter with him again makes me nervous. Like I know he's gonna get ornery. He don't disappoint me, either.

"'Do you want the body?' the girl asks him.

"'Of course not,' he snaps. 'We don't eat dog.'"

His younger brother, Leroy, comes in shortly after. He's the same build as Lionel, only heavier. More like a light-heavyweight. Plus he has his hair yet. Lionel pulls up his shirt and shows Leroy his scar. Like a red welt from a whip, though it's healing nicely. A few more regulars also stop at our booth to talk to Lionel, none of who pay me much notice. So, by the time it's my round, I'm feeling easier. More like I'm in somebody else's local, as opposed to some exotic watering hole.

Next thing I know, there's a clip of the parade in New York on the Six O'Clock News behind the bar.

"You want me to ask Porky," Lionel grins, "has he any green beer?"

"Maybe a shot of Old Thompson," I say, "before I go."

Lionel gets me that, plus a small draft beer to chase it. Given the day that's in it, I lower the OT into the beer, shot glass and all. Like Sean Hickey used to do Friday nights, after a week on a building site.

"A Boilermaker," I tell Lionel. "You want one?"

"I start that shit," says Lionel, "and I'll never get home." I get him another bottle of Schlitz so, and we take our time. Seeing as neither of us is going to start that shit.

"You locked the bay doors?" Lionel suddenly asks. Only I know he's just trying to wind me up.

"You have your set of keys," I remind him. "And it's on your head if ever they're unlocked."

"Fintan had it right," Lionel says. "Cat told me he wouldn't keep a job that had more than two keys."

"Fintan couldn't keep a job, full-stop."

"You got that right."

"Was it the dope?" I suddenly ask.

"Dope?" Lionel laughs out loud. "Shit, weed's all the dope Fintan did."

Still laughing, he fishes inside the front pocket of his pea coat on the seat beside him. Pulling out a sandwich bag of what looks like a few tablespoons of Maggie's herbs. Oregano maybe.

"You want me to turn you on, Mickey? Just a weed. Grass. Grow it in a garden, right up your alley!"

"I'll stick to what I know," I lift my glass.

"That's cool," says Lionel, putting the baggie back into his coat.

"That ain't my stash," he adds, "case you think I'm lighting up on the job. My son bought this coat last month, and I only got it away from him this morning. I might have a toke weekends, but that's about it. 'You're not in the Army now,' Diane says, any time she sees me lighting up."

He tells this story then of Vietnam. Of being posted to a combat motor pool somewhere north of Saigon. "It'd been real quiet for a couple of days, so a few of us dropped acid this night, thinking it'd be safe enough. We're just getting off, when Charlie decides to throw a party for us. A big fucking party, with mortars, and tracer fire. And flares bursting overhead, only real slow, like that time-lapse photography shit they do on flowers? Where you see the petals opening up? 'Cept the colours when you're tripping are something else. Blues and reds bleeding across the sky. Meanwhile all hell's broken loose inside the compound. Everybody racing round with their M-16s, looking to see has Charlie breached the perimeter. It don't seem safe somehow, so we crawl under this big transport truck, and lie there to watch the show."

Lionel goes to the jacks then. Coming back, he unbuttons his dark blue work shirt, with *Lionel* stitched above the pocket in red thread. "Dig this, Mickey," he says, pointing to a black tee-shirt with a pint of Guinness on it, beside which I read IRELAND — 40 SHADES OF BLACK.

"Well, you're one shade anyhow," I laugh, asking him where he got it.

"From Fintan, where else? Last summer, saying I oughta wear it for you on Patrick's Day."

Maybe it's the buzz from the Boilermaker, but suddenly it's like I've stepped back inside my head. Stepped back to see myself seated in a bar booth, with this black guy across the table. Like it's something I've done every day of my life. Lionel starts telling another story about his Pappy, but suddenly I'm remembering an even closer encounter last week inside the Central Square subway station. Going downtown to get a new pair of work shoes in Filene's. There is a massive turnstile in the station, just down from the booth where JoJo used to sit. Like a revolving door, only it's partitioned by racks of iron bars instead of glass. Anyhow, this coloured kid either tried to get a free ride by slipping in behind me, or else his token jammed. Either way, the turnstile stuck, and there was the two of us crammed into the one cage, like feeding time at the zoo. I could feel the kid pressed up behind me, and I could smell coconut oil too.

"Ease back," I told him, while I pulled on the bars in front. It took a few tries to free it up, but we got out onto the platform just as the train pulled in.

I looked at the kid. Around seventeen or so, trying to act like having been behind bars was nothing he couldn't handle. Though he hadn't even his sneakers laced. Wearing a Georgetown jacket, which is probably as close to a college as he'll ever get. Plus this haircut which made his head look like a box-hedge. Sides shaved close, but high and flat on top.

"What's happening, Pops?" he said.

"It don't make no never mind," I replied. Using the few words of English I've learned off Lionel so far. But the kid's running for the next subway car already, before I could slap him five.

Lionel and I talk some more about Fintan. And, just before I get up to go, I finally learn about the bowling team thing.

"Fintan was living in Arizona," Lionel says, the coloured barlights reflecting off his shaved head. "Had a tit job with this huge diesel outfit. Plenty of overtime, dental care, even a bowling team."

"How'd he mess that up?" I ask. "Boozing?"

"Hell no," Lionel laughs. "Crazy dude thought it *was* messed up!"

"I don't follow," I say.

"Fintan said the whole setup freaked him out. Like he couldn't handle living in this flash apartment, having a closetful of new clothes. Plus central-air and a swimming pool."

"He threw it up?"

"Not just that, but he pushes his car off a cliff. And throws his clothes after it, plus a brand-new bowling ball."

"His car?"

"Second-hand Honda, but still!"

"Puzzle me that?" I say.

"Go figure," says Lionel.

There's slush underfoot walking home. But on Pearl Street someone has started to knock down a garden wall, and the spindly irons rods leaning out of the concrete rubble put me in mind of spring. Of the first grass poking up from a newly sown lawn. And spring is officially just three days away, even if it started six weeks ago in Ireland. Where Fintan said they always had their spuds in the ground by Paddy's Day. I remember thinking at one point last summer that maybe

Fintan would take over the garage. "Thinking Disneyland," as Lionel would say. Foolish, that — as if Fintan were my kid or something. What's more likely is my selling out to Lionel in a couple of years. And why not, if he wants it? For Lucy certainly won't. At least I'm not imagining Lionel's my brother. Even if he's better crack than Jack. And I'd love to see Sal's face, who used to puzzle over selling out to the Irish, had he thought a coloured might end up with the garage?

Still, the place helped keep me on the rails over here. Or not so much on the rails as rooted in the one place? Garage and garden both, for that matter. And, if stuck in Cambridge, at least not stuck somewhere in between. Like JoJo, crying in his beer about Sligo on a summer's night. Or Fintan, unable to square Donegal with a permanent & pensionable slot in Arizona. Though maybe it's just human nature, to want to be always elsewhere? Even my Da, who never set foot outside Ireland, reading up on the bird market in Barcelona. Turning onto our street, I think again of Fintan, wondering might he return come spring? At heart, however, I know he was more a once-off annual than a perennial, poking its head up every year. Or, better yet, a "garden escape" — like the fuchsia, first planted at Irish big houses, that now grows wild everywhere.

Acknowledgements

The author would like to thank David Marcus, who published the germ of this novel as a short story, 'Transplants', in **Phoenix Irish Short Stories 1997**, and Dermot Bolger, who suggested that it might grow into something more. Thanks also to Paco, John, Mark, Rene, and the two Mickeys, master mechanics all.